Praise for *Nine*

"Paula Bomer is one of those scary-talented writers and upsets and provokes in about equal measure, yet her work remains deeply funny and infused with a certain cock-eyed hopefulness. *Nine Months* is the best book I have read about the secret fears and sinister underbelly of becoming a parent, a satire which should be viewed not only as a stellar novel, bit as as a challenge to a literary scene mired in laziness, backslapping and lousy clichés."

—Tony O'Neill, author of *Sick City*

"Bold, transgressive and overtly sexual. There have been countless road novels, but none about a hormonally driven pregnant mother in search of her soul. Eye-opening! Shocking! Satisfying!"

—Thelma Adams, author of *Playdate*

"Paul Bomer's *Nine Months* is a daring look at motherhood, exploring the thoughts most women keep secret. Sonia's journey begins with her dumping her sons' two empty child's car seats by the road in the dark in an attempt to flee a sense of being caged in, a sense that some part of herself and her dreams were pushed aside for too long, were pushed, in fact, to the brink. Bold, alarming, provocative! A page-turner that will tie your stomach in knots and stir up one hell of a debate.

—Susan Henderson, author of *Up from the Blue*

"Paula Bomer's debut novel is so many things: shocking and engrossing, funny and sad. *Nine Months* begins with wholesome playdates in the park—and then goes deliciously, dangerously rogue. Sometimes, I wanted to shake pregnant Sonia, mother of two small children, and seemingly model citizen of Brooklyn. I always wanted to keep turning the pages, desperate to see what she would do next."

—Marcy Dermansky, author of *Bad Marie*

"*Nine Months* is hilarious, fearless, and totally original. Paula Bomer holds nothing back in this page-turning account of love, sex, pregnancy, marriage and motherhood. Bomer could have titled this work *What to REALLY Expect When You're Expecting* as there is more raw, honest truth in this novel than any parenting book I've ever read."

—Jessica Anya Blau, author of *Drinking Closer to Home*

Praise for Paula Bomer

"Words like 'tough' and 'honest' don't quite do justice to the fiction of Paula Bomer. These stories bleed, yes, but that's because they brawl. The real housewives of Bomerworld break themselves and break your heart and yet never completely lose their soulful dignity."

—Sam Lipsyte, author of *The Ask*

"I love that Paula Bomer writes her characters into difficult situations and does terrible things to them. These stories contain a rare emotional honesty and brutality."

—Michael Kimball, author of *Dear Everybody*

"[Bomer] lands firmly between Mary Gaitskill's articulate, unflinching anhedonia and Kathy Acker... Amy Hempel with a twist of Grace Paley."   —*Bookforum*

nine months

months

a novel

paula bomer

SOHO

for Mark Doten, the true believer,
and for Nick, my love

Portions of this novel appeared in altered form in Nerve and Dogzplot

Published by
Soho Press, Inc.
853 Broadway
New York, NY 10003

Library of Congress Cataloging-in-Publication Data
Bomer, Paula.
Nine months / Paula Bomer.
p. cm.
ISBN 978-1-61695-146-7
eISBN 978-1-61695-147-4
1. Pregnant women—Fiction. 2. Husband and wife—Ficiton.
3. Life change events—Fiction. I. Title.
PS3602.O653N56 2012
813'.6—dc23
2012010156

Interior design by Janine Agro, Soho Press, Inc.

Printed in the United States of America

10 9 8 7 6 5 4 3 2 1

So squeezed, wince you I scream? I love you & hate
off with you. Ages! Useless. Below my waist
he has me in Hell's vise.
Stalling. He let go. Come back: brace
me somewhere. No. No. Yes! everything down
hardens I press with horrible joy down
my back cracks like a wrist
shame I am voiding oh behind it is too late

hide me forever I work thrust I must free
now I all muscles & bones concentrate
what is living from dying?
Simon I must leave you so untidy
Monster you are killing me Be sure
I'll have you later Women do endure
I can can no longer
and it passes the wretched trap whelming and I am me

drencht & powerful. I did it with my body!

—JOHN BERRYMAN

In my coat of many colors
I'm waiting for my child
I'm waiting for my journey
I'm waiting for my prize

My Lord, My Lord.

—PJ HARVEY, "Long Time Coming"

1

February 7

"**I**DID IT!" She screams, "I DID IT WITH MY OWN BODY!" Her voice is ungodly deep. The veins in her neck thick with blood. And it's true. Her body, once more, did it. What's left of it. Bleeding, bloated, bruised inside and out. Ripped and torn, the yellowish, green umbilical cord resembling some sort of proof that aliens do indeed exist, they exist inside of our very bodies. The slimy, luminescent cord is proof of universal mystery, this strange device that attached her to her daughter—it's from inside of her body, just like her daughter, too, the red-faced infant screaming in the doctor's arms. Her insides came out. It's the end of the world.

Because each time it happens, she swears, never again, never again, even as she holds the tiny infant that, unbelievably, unfuckingbelievably, grew inside of her. She's in awe of her daughter, in awe and also, not so oddly, rather unmoved by her. She feels no love, just wonder. No love surges forth, like it did with Mike her youngest (but not with Tom, it's like it was with Tom, the confusion, the mystery). Funny, bluish, screamy wormlike thing. She puts her on her left breast and prods at the little baby's mouth to take the nipple. The baby's mouth roots around like a baby bird, unable to grasp on. So Sonia squeezes her nipple and colostrum comes out and the infant's lips touch the pre-milk milk and then, it works—the baby tries to suck. First slowly, and then, as if something in her wired-for-survival brain clicks, she ferociously latches on to Sonia's nipple and sucks on her like that's what she's been put on this earth to do. Which is, in fact, true. Her daughter is here to suck the life out of her, and leave her for the spent, middle-aged woman she soon will be. Nothing will be remotely the same again. No one has ever threatened Sonia as much as this unnamed infant. No one has ever made it clear how useless and spent she really is.

She grew her, like she grew Tom and Mike. Like a plant, but inside of her, and with a brain, too. Sonia stares at the doctor for a minute. How can someone do this for a living? How can they do this for a living, watch women turn themselves inside out, and not have nervous breakdowns? It's not that different than being a gravedigger. It's just not. And then, Sonia, still deflating like a balloon, as a large liver-like placenta hurtles out of her, starts shaking with pain. Her teeth chatter. Her vision blurs. Is this the part where she dies? That was supposed to be earlier, thinks Sonia. The nurse, Beatrice, who is once again a normal, nice nurse—this, after Sonia saw her with that hallucinatory vision, with rainbows surrounding her and light glowing around her head, she had a fucking halo, she *did*, Sonia was sure of it—now this nurse is just a nice, normal nurse and gives Sonia a shot of Demoral in her thigh to stop the shakes.

"Sometimes people shake real badly with the postbirth contractions," Beatrice says. "The fluid leaving them so quickly sets the body off into convulsions. You'll be fine. It's nothing abnormal. Nothing to be worried about."

Sonia was in love with this woman only a few hours ago. And she still likes her, but now she *just* likes her. The magic is gone. Nothing abnormal? Everything is abnormal. There is nothing normal about what Sonia just went through. There is no normal.

BUT THAT WAS LATER. First, there was more driving to be done. Sitting with her pregnant self in the black leather bucket seat of her Volkswagen Passat station wagon.

It just crept up on her. She was never so lucky, with any of her kids, as to have the drama of her water breaking. No, for about two weeks really, her lower body ached, and then hurt, really hurt, increasingly so. For two weeks, she felt so tired, so exhausted, with intermittent sharp headaches,

that whenever she walked, even the littlest bit—from the
hotel room to the car, from the front seat of the car to the
McDonald's, from the parking lot to the mall—she felt as
if she couldn't go on. Just physically moving her big body
drained her utterly. She wanted to lie down. But then, as
soon as she lay down, she wanted to move again. She was
never comfortable.

Exhausted restlessness. Bothness. It was time. It was
going to happen soon.

SHE'S BEEN DRIVING EAST for some time. She missed
Christmas, which was the guiltiest pleasure of all, but the
guilt almost ruined the pleasure. No wrapping presents.
No buying presents for anyone. No in-laws. No decorat-
ing a tree. No goddamn cards to mail out. No having to
do a million things at preschool. No singing. No special
meals to prepare for her ungrateful family. No pretending that she lives for trying to make everyone happy, when
no one noticed that she wasn't happy herself, that she
really didn't give a fuck. She didn't believe in Jesus Christ
anyway. She didn't believe that the son of God came and
saved everyone's souls, or just those who prayed to Him.
Although, she did pray, just in case, because even though
she didn't believe in Jesus Christ, she didn't believe there
wasn't anything out there. She prayed desperately to the
random molecules to be kind to her. But Jesus? No. And
yet, they were Christians in some vague, historical way,

Dick and she, and they played the whole game. Told them-selves it was about the kids. Every Christmas, they gave five hundred dollars to City Meals on Wheels and bought a ton of cheap plastic toys that made the boys freak out for about two days. It depressed her. It made her feel oddly guilty, an empty sort of false joy and yet the boys were genuinely happy, wasn't that enough?

This Christmas she spent laying her fat butt down at a Ramada Inn in Nebraska, watching TV and eating bags of chips and boxes of créme-filled oatmeal cookies. She fell asleep with the TV on. For some reason, she didn't feel depressed and guilty about that. She felt guilty because she did nothing that she was supposed to do anymore. Missing Christmas was like having her very own Christmas for the first time since Tom was born five years ago. But the guilt was a wicked tongue telling her that she really was the devil. Jesus held no sway with Sonia, but evil was a scary force one saw on a regular basis. And who's to say it wasn't inside of her? For weeks and weeks now, the guilt ate at her as she ate her way around America. Her conscience spoke to her, and it told her horrible stuff about herself. She'd listen, and then move on. She wasn't a monster as long as her conscience spoke, she reasoned. As long as she had a conscience, she wasn't actually the worst person on earth, she was just rebel-ling. Or so she told herself. But everyone knows a mother who leaves her children is the worst thing on earth; a sinner, a loser, a person whose life isn't worth living.

She missed New Years. Happy New Year! On New Year's Eve, she fell asleep at 10 P.M. in a Motel 6 in Illinois. But now, in the gloom of February, now she heads back. Because the baby is coming. And, guilt or no guilt, she has no control over what she has to do now. It was a relief, actually, the lack of responsibility. She has no choice in the matter. She has to push this baby out.

WHEN SHE WALKS AROUND the malls that she haunts, she walks so slowly, like the baby's head is right there, right above her vagina, like there is a bowling ball between her legs. She positively waddles. And it feels like a bowling ball is leaning on her crotch. It fucking hurts. How much does a bowling ball weigh? How much does this baby, the placenta, the extra pints and pints of blood and fluid weigh? The same as a bowling ball? Probably more. Sometimes, a sharp stabbing pain. Other times, just a dull throbbing that becomes like some horrible white noise; at first she ignores the pain and then it's the only thing she can think of. So she sits down on a bench across from the indoor fountains at the mall—throb, throb, throb.

She's due. And, like the other two times, she's in denial. Because, who after all wants to deal with that pain? Who wants to welcome the horror that is birth? Who joyfully embraces the thought of their body cleaving in two? Vague, nightmarish memories of the other births startle her, flash at her, as she does her thing, the driving, the walking around malls, the walking from her car to a gas station and then back again, the lying around hotel rooms. Meanwhile, she pretends this isn't her labor very slowly starting. But it is. At a mall in Michigan, after eating an enormous steak and a baked potato for dinner—she never eats the potato, why now?—she waddles out to her station wagon and gets in the car and heads toward New York. Not vaguely east. No, now she drives straight for New York City, straight for Brooklyn. She drives eighty miles an hour most of the time. She's anxious. She wants to get there. She's heading back to her boys. To her man. The father of this baby.

But she doesn't quite make it. She's not a confident driver to begin with. When her stomach hardens up, it becomes hard to focus on the road. She can still see the road. In fact, morning's pushing through, hazy and dark, a dark February morning, and she knows she's been sitting in this car for that long now—and she's been in Pennsylvania for a long time. God, she's close, but the hardening of her stomach, the *contraction*—the word actually presents itself to her—is telling her to pull over and ask where the nearest hospital is.

"Twenty minutes to downtown Philadelphia," the man at the gas station tells her. Twenty minutes. She can do it. They are coming faster now, the contractions, regularly, too. Her first labor was eleven hours, not bad. Her second was eight hours long. How long would this one be? She has more than twenty minutes before the baby forces herself out, she must. She says to herself, "I've got at least a few hours. I've got time. Drive slow, breathe," and she talks to herself like this until she enters Philly, a city she's only been to once or twice with her family, long ago. Once, they stayed in a hotel and went swimming in the indoor pool and then walked around, sightseeing. What was the second time? She can't remember now, the pain during her contractions distracting her memory for the most part. She does remember where the man told her to go and she makes the turns and there's the hospital.

She is the only white person in the waiting area. After talking to the triage nurse, she's sent out to give her insurance card to the person at the desk and then she's ushered out of the emergency waiting room into another room right away. Ahead of all the dark-skinned people. She wishes this was because she's about to have a baby, but she knows it's because she has a good insurance card. Once, when Mike had a horrible ear infection, she took him to the emergency room in a downtown Brooklyn hospital and the look on their faces when she produced her insurance card! It was as if she were holding out a bar of gold for payment.

They have a room in their maternity ward. The nurse Beatrice comes in, a West Indian woman by her accent. She checks her pulse. She listens to the baby's heartbeat with a long corded thing. She times her contractions. "They're three minutes apart, but they're not lasting very long. They don't feel that powerful, do they?"

"No, not really."

"The doctor will be here soon to see how dilated you are."

A handsome, middle-aged white woman appears. She looks tired, but she smiles. She introduces herself as Dr. Lumiere and then says, "Let's take a look at you then."

She puts her hand deep inside of Sonia's crotch. This hurts. She moves her hand around and Sonia can feel the hand twisting inside of her and she can see the doctor's arm from the elbow up, moving this way and that. The doctor's face held in concentration. Seeing with her fingers. "Where are you from?"

"Brooklyn."

"Your husband's not here?"

"He's in Brooklyn."

"You've had two other deliveries, I noticed from your chart."

"I have two kids, yes."

"And where are they?"

"They're in Brooklyn. With their father."

Suddenly, the hospital gown held loosely over her breasts and enormous stomach feels incredibly inadequate. Sonia feels ashamed. "I was heading back to Brooklyn from a business trip and didn't quite make it." She smiles. She's a horrible liar. She fruitlessly tries to pull the crinkly gown over her body to hide her shame, but it doesn't work.

"Have you called them? They could make it here on time." The doctor finally pulls her hand out of Sonia.

"How dilated am I?"

"You're only three centimeters dilated, but you're completely effaced. This being your third birth, it shouldn't be that long. I'll get the anesthesiologist on call."

"I don't want an epidural. I didn't get one with my other kids."

The doctor looks at her critically.

"If the nurse can give me a shot of Demoral, I'll be fine. Really. I prefer Demoral. I like drugs that mess with my head better than the ones that just numb you."

"Would you get a tooth pulled without the numbing pain reliever?"

"No. But I'm not getting a tooth pulled. I'm having a baby." And if I were getting my tooth pulled, thinks Sonia, I'd ask for the gas, too. It's like doing whippets.

"But getting a tooth pulled isn't nearly as painful as giving birth. And it doesn't make sense that you'd get numbing pain reliever for pulling a tooth but not for having a baby. There's no reason to feel all that pain."

"I'm one of those weird people who kind of gets off on pain, OK?"

"You really should have someone here with you. A sister or your mother, if you're not going to call your husband.

We can't really let you leave unless you have someone here to take you home."

"Well, I just got here so let's not think about me leaving yet. I just got here."

Dr. Lumiere frowns at her. Sonia feels high. The endorphins, in reaction to the contractions, must have just kicked in. She gets a rush to her head. She says, "You're beautiful when you frown."

"Are you on any medication? Lithium? Prozac?"

"No," she says.

"No high blood pressure, no diabetes . . ."

"Oh, no, nothing like that. I'm healthy."

"When was your last prenatal checkup?"

"I'm not sure."

"Were you having weekly checkups?"

"It was a while ago, my last checkup. It was a couple months ago."

Dr. Lumiere frowns again. "Well, everything looks fine."

THE ROOM IS SMALLER than the one she had both her boys in. Both of her boys were delivered in the same room at the same beautiful maternity ward in Manhattan. But although the room is small, it has a nice view and it's clean. Sonia is happy. The nurse comes and checks her contractions again. They've slowed down, they're now five minutes apart, but they're getting deeper. She can really feel them, they pull at her, and she stops thinking about other things—about her boys, about her husband, about Phil Rush, the man, her old professor, she's just come from visting—and just feels the pain.

The nurse says, "Your contractions have slowed down. Probably because you're more relaxed now. You've been lying down for a while. It's OK. Don't worry. This baby's coming today."

Today? *Today?* God, she's going to have a baby, she's going to give birth, a fucking baby is going to come out of her, a person. Another goddamn person. She shudders. The nice nurse may know the baby is coming, and may tell this to Sonia, but Sonia doesn't believe it, exactly. She is suddenly struck with the enormity of it all. The panic it causes her to think of it! So she just stops thinking about it. That pain that she's feeling? She'd rather be in her pain, right now—*live for the moment!*—than think about what's ahead.

Sonia gets up from her bed. She puts on a robe from a bag of mall clothing she's acquired on this trip. A huge, gray maternity robe. She shoves her feet into the hospital slippers, flimsy, paper things, and decides to walk around the building a bit, to fend off her thoughts. In the hallway, at the nurse's station, she asks Beatrice if they sell good slippers, fluffy slippers, at the gift shop.

"I'm not sure. You could take a look, though."

Sonia walks toward the elevator. A contraction comes

and she stops for a moment, puts her hand on her belly. Her stomach gets hard as a rock, it's like a smooth, rounded stone, and Sonia stands there and feels it. It hurts nicely, purposefully, rightly. And then it's gone. And she's in the elevator.

The gift shop isn't so bad. Really. Some T-shirts, some cheap jewelry. Coffee mugs. No slippers though. Sonia thinks of talking to the woman behind the desk about how slippers would be a good thing to carry in the hospital seeing as how the slippers the hospital gives you aren't very nice. They barely stay on your feet. But as she smilingly walks toward the saleswoman the woman glares at her and Sonia decides against giving her any advice. She decides against striking up a conversation with this woman. This woman doesn't want to talk to her.

And who does, really? Is that why she keeps having kids, so someone will want to talk to her? Someone had said to her once, people have kids so they don't have to deal with making friends. You have kids and they have to be your friends, or, at the very least, your company, your human interaction, as they live with you and off of you for years and years. God, how she misses her boys. And Dick. Yes, and Dick.

BACK ON THE MATERNITY ward, Beatrice comes and checks her out. The nurse's skin is a very dark brown and there is something creamy about her skin, something smooth and perfect. Sonia can tell she's young. In her twenties. She gives Sonia her attention. She doesn't seem hurried or angry or burned out. This is good luck, thinks Sonia, this means that everything is going to be OK. This nice, energetic nurse is a premonition, is grace from God. Everything is going to be OK! My boys, my marriage. This creature inside me. Sonia could have just as easily gotten a bitter, nasty, exhausted woman who hates her job. But no, Sonia was given this woman, whose nametag says Beatrice, this young, fresh-faced beautiful woman smiling at her this very moment. Whose hands are gentle and cool and very soft and smell lightly of Jergen's lotion. Beatrice times her contractions and says, "Let's get the doctor in here again. Your contractions are longer now."

Dr. Lumiere comes in, with Beatrice behind her. Sonia is standing at the window right now, looking down to the streets ten floors below. The pain, when it comes, and now it is always coming, makes her face go slack, her mouth open. A bit of drool drops to the floor. Walking around, walking down to the gift shop, must have helped things along. "Come lie down for a minute, so we can check you again."

Sonia obeys. Dr. Lumiere puts her fist inside Sonia again and concentrates.

"Do you have any kids, Dr. Lumiere?"

"Yes, one boy. He's eleven now. It's a lot of work." She

smiles, but it's not Beatrice's smile. "I was much older than you when I had him. I'd been a doctor for so long. It was a big change. I love him to pieces, but it's a lot of work. It is. We have full-time help. Although he's getting kind of old for that."

"I wish I were a doctor. Or something. I wish I weren't home as much as I am. I think I'd be happier."

"You've gone another centimeter. Things are moving. I could really get things going by stripping your membranes."

The thought of getting her membranes stripped, of getting her water broken, hurts. Her contractions hurt, but once the water's gone, the pain hits directly on the pelvic bone, hard. Everything moves so fast then. It'll all be over. "No, no, please don't." There's fear in her voice. "It'll hurt so much."

"Why don't you let me give you an epidural? There's still time."

"Just let it go naturally, if possible." Sonia hears fear in her voice. Pleading. She doesn't want a needle in her spine, even if it means she won't feel a thing. She doesn't want her water broken either, which is really silly, she knows, because it's going to break any minute now anyway. She wants to be left alone, is what she wants.

"Well, you're going to have this baby soon enough anyway," the doctor says impatiently.

"I need to be alone for a minute." Sonia asks quietly

and they leave her and she goes to the window again. Oh, the pain. The contractions bear down on her now, the doctor's fist having changed things again, having loosened things up down there, and her knees are weak with pain. Her mouth opens. Oh, Jesus, what is happening? Can this really be happening? And again, a big one, and Sonia falls to her knees now, holding on to the window sill. It's going to happen. They're right. And she's alone, in fucking Philadelphia. But that's OK. It's how it should be. She doesn't want him here anyway and she certainly doesn't want her boys here. One friend of hers, Marisa, had her five-year-old daughter watch when she gave birth to her second child. She wanted to share the experience with her daughter. Sonia found that idea very confusing. Who would want to share this with a little girl? Or a little boy? Or with anyone, for that matter? Here, in a strange town, with complete strangers, this is the way Sonia always wanted to give birth. Yes, yes, it is a part of life. But it's not a pretty part of life. She doesn't take a shit in front of her kids or husband, either. And giving birth equals taking a shit, and then some. And then a lot more. And the pain, the transforming pain—who would want to show a little girl her own mother, mentally insane with pain? The blood, the pain, the shit. No, children may not be as innocent as the world wants them to be, but this, but *birth*, is for grown ups.

The first moan escapes. It's a quiet one. She leans her

head down on her belly, down between her knees. She's squatting now and for some reason, this feels good for a moment. Squatting in a hospital room by herself, the sun barely visible through the window, the gray streets and sky of Philadelphia in February. And yet, it's just this moment that she needs, a clear moment, a moment where the vise grip of her own body lets go, so she can think for a minute, everything is OK, everything is OK. I'm going to be OK. And then another contraction.

Sonia falls forward. She's on her hands and knees now and she moans louder. She moans through the contraction. She gets up then, when it's subsiding, not really over, but almost, and she throws herself on the hospital bed. She curls up in a fetal position for a moment. Then, it's that time when she needs to be totally naked. She's hot. Her body is like an oven. So the maternity robe lands on the ground. Her body is her enemy now. It's hot, it's huge, it's doing weird things to itself. It's not recognizable and it fucking hurts like hell. Now, now is when Sonia knows that there is a God and he doesn't love her. He doesn't love her because she, after all, is not a good person. Not a good mother, not a good wife, not a good daughter and not a good sister. And that is why the pain feels so right, because she deserves this pain. She deserves this message from God. And she feels blessed. She feels in communion with God, she feels he is letting her suffer, letting her burn in the hell that is her body, her burning body, and it all makes sense. Karma. What goes around, comes around. She deserves this pain. It is the pain she has caused to others, coming back to say hello.

And then another quiet moment. Sonia feels weak, spent, shaken. Yet, she can see clearly. She runs to the little bathroom in her room and shit pours out of her, as if she's had an enema, which she had the first time around, and not the second, because, like now, it just all came out of her. Her head is in her hands, her elbows on her knees, and her head feels cold and clammy. She goes and gets the robe off the floor and wraps it around her for a second. Beatrice comes in. "How're you doing?" The smile. The real smile, a genuine kindness expressed for a total stranger. The knowing smile that says, you're going to have a baby.

"I don't know how you do this." Sonia voice sounds strange, not deep yet, but almost vibrato. "How can you watch this?"

"I'm not doing anything, you're the one doing the work here."

"But how can you stand it?" Tears stream down her face and she moans and stoops over the bed, moving back and forth as another contraction bears down on her. "Damn. Damn it hurts."

"I can see if it's not too late for an epidural."

"No, no I deserve this. I deserve it all."

"What's that?" Now Beatrice is on her, rubbing her back

and arms, wiping her brow. "You don't deserve anything. Don't torture yourself. You're having a baby."

"I don't know if I want this baby. I really don't," says Sonia and then a trickling down her leg. Her water broke, all on its own. Slowly, it's coming down her legs. No big gush. No fountain of water.

"Oh, look. Your water's broken. And it's clear. That's good. But I better get Dr. Lumiere."

Dr. Lumiere arrives and Sonia sees her for the bitch she is. She's pissed that Sonia isn't on the bed with an epidural in her spine. She's pissed that Sonia is being difficult in general, and perhaps, understandably, she doesn't want to deliver this baby, this baby whose father isn't here, whose mother doesn't live here. She seems, in fact, like a lot of professional women in their fifties—pissed off and ready to retire. Yes, maybe it's not just Sonia's baby that's the problem, but delivering babies in general.

Sonia asks, "How long did you say you've been doing this?" as the doctor listens to the baby's heartbeat.

"A long time." And the smile again, the curt, professional smile. "Well, things are moving along. How are you feeling?"

"I need some water. I just shit my brains out. I don't feel so great."

"The baby's heartbeat is fine. It's doing fine."

Another contraction bears down on Sonia and she rolls over on the bed, away from the other two women and tries to stifle a scream. She doesn't stifle it. She screams. The doctor walks out and Beatrice comes up to Sonia.

"Oh, you're a screamer, huh? That's all right. Just scream if you need to, if it makes you feel better." Beatrice says this as she rubs Sonia's spine, the spine that faces her now.

"Yeah, yeah I'm a screamer," Sonia says, her voice changing now, really changing, deep and breathless. "Oh God. Help me God. Oh God." And then she stands up, her eyes wild with fear. "It hurts now. It hurts so badly. I don't want to push this baby out. I don't want to do it. I'M SCARED. I'M SCARED OF THE PAIN. I'M SCARED THE BABY WON'T BE OK. I'M SCARED OF MEETING THIS BABY." And then another one hits her and she falls on her hands and knees and rocks back and forth, back and forth.

Beatrice crouches next to her, the constant rubbing of her smooth, soft hands. The creamy skin and sane touch on Sonia's sweating, crazed body. "Why are you scared? What are scared about? This baby's going to be fine. All the tests came back fine, right? That's what's on the chart, sweetheart. Everything's going to be fine. You're doing a great job. You're almost done. You're almost done."

Sonia's mind hits another clear spot. Suddenly, it sees outside herself. The little bathroom. The table with medical equipment. She looks behind her. There's the window. And then, in her clearness, she feels bile rise and she rushes for the little bathroom, not quite making it to the toilet, and vomits on the floor, on the clean white tiles of the bathroom floor. There goes her steak and her baked potato. She sees it and it confuses her, as it all seems so long ago. "I'm sorry. I'm so sorry."

"That's alright, don't worry. I'll clean it up," says Beatrice and she goes out to get a bucket and rags and Sonia is ashamed and grateful and doesn't want Beatrice to leave her. "Don't leave me!" She cries as Beatrice heads out the door. "Don't leave me! I need you!"

And Beatrice says, "I'll be right back. Don't worry, I'll be right back," and her voice is calm and creamy like her skin, comforting Sonia, and Sonia loves this woman with a power beyond her. She loves Beatrice and sees the glow now, the halo around this nurse, and she feels a moment of euphoria. She's been blessed! Beatrice is the angel sent from above to shepherd her through this time! Sonia lays herself down on the bed, on her side, and curls up, again, in a fetal position. She pants, but everything is clear now. She's having a baby. She's going to push out a baby. And she closes her eyes and takes a deep breath.

Later, when the pushing starts, the top half of Sonia will try and run away from the lower half. With one final burst of energy, she'll roll over on her hands and knees, from where she was on her back getting ready to push the baby out, and she will try and crawl away from herself. Something she's been trying to do her whole life, really. But it doesn't work. Gravity, reality, her body and soul, throws her back on her back, knees splayed, heaving stomach before bulging eyes, and like a volcano splitting the earth's skin, her daughter comes out.

2

June—eight months earlier

Sonia doesn't want another baby. She doesn't want another abortion, either. She's had two babies and one abortion already. In the darkness of her bedroom bathroom—she's in too much of a hurry to turn the light on—at the crack of dawn, she struggles to open the plastic wrapper. Her knees tightly together, wiggling her butt around so she doesn't pee in her underpants (God, she has to pee so badly, the feeling is abnormally intense, as if she just drank a case of beer, a pretty sure sign she's pregnant), and then—there, she's got it—she sits and releases a stream of piss onto the white stick. She manages to urinate all over her hand as well as she sits awkwardly scrunched over the toilet. She makes a face in disgust and holds her peed-on hand stiffly. Pee on her hand is not a new thing, as the mother of two small children. Pee, poop, spit-up, saliva-ridden cookie bits. This is her life. Tom is four.

Michael is two. He's still in diapers! He just started talking well, really well, actually, and she's so relieved to be done with that stage where all they can do is cry to express themselves. Soon the diapers will be gone, too, as long as she doesn't fuck it up by getting too intense about toilet training, something she learned the hard way from Tom. Her children are little, yes, but she has no babies! And she's very happy about that. Smug, even. When she's in the playground and sees another mother with an infant at the breast or in her arms, she thinks, ha, I'm over that. I'm done with all that. Now that both her kids sleep through the night, sit at a table (more or less) and stick their own food into their own mouths, life is much, much better. Now that she isn't so exhausted anymore, now that she and Dick go to the movies once a week, now that they like each other better than they have since Tom was first born four long, wrinkle-inducing years ago, now that they are fucking again, now, now it's all going to go away?

This hard-earned, long-awaited breather. Her children are too small to cause real trouble, being past the crying, run-into-traffic, eat-crap-off the-floor, constantly teething stage. The green, tree-lined streets of Brooklyn produce an air that smells sweeter than ever, as she can now bring a magazine to the playgrounds and relax, really *relax*, while her two boys play nicely on the low, super safely designed, modern jungle gyms. Her legs look good again, the bulging pregnancy veins having mostly receded. She's been feeling hopeful. She isn't drowning in laundry. And now it's all going away? Now this?

Because, frankly, Sonia and Dick still feel young. Sonia's thirty-five and Dick's thirty-eight. They wanted to learn tennis together. To go to museums. To wear stylish clothing that won't get spit-up on it. Just not to bend over constantly! To not worry about their boys falling down the stairs or eating broken glass. They want a little bit of *freedom*. And they have been tasting it now for a few months, because when Mike turned two, things just started to feel easier. They've had the talk about how they specifically want only two children, so they can still afford to live in the city, still get by with a decently spacious two-bedroom apartment. No pressing need for a big house and yard. Yes, they've just started seeing a movie once a week. But Sonia wants to start painting again, too. She wants to stick Mike in preschool in the mornings in the fall (he was already signed up) and do whatever the fuck she wants to do, which is, primarily, to paint.

Before she moved to New York, before she met Dick, fell in love, got married and then, right away, pregnant (because face it, waiting until you're forty to have a baby is *stupid*), before she became who she is now, a tired housewife with a bad haircut, before that, she painted. And nothing else really mattered to her. She lived in Boston, slept with lots of men, drank a lot, and painted constantly. Day and night. She painted until her soul ached, and then she painted some more. She painted until the painting was good, and then she kept painting until the painting sucked, and then she painted some more. She had what they called dedication. Or a calling. She made little time for socializing, but she did fuck a lot. She fucked not one, not two, but three of her professors at the Museum School in Boston. And all this, without being beautiful or having large breasts. Her professors fucked her because she knew how to paint and it turned them on, or so she believed and still believes. OK, being young helped. But would Philbert Rush, famous abstract painter extraordinaire, really have fucked her just because she was twenty-two? He fucked her because he thought she was talented, too. Sonia loves her boys, loves them more than anything, but she's been patiently waiting for this time to come. The time of no babies. Children are one thing, babies another.

And Dick talked about quitting his job, doing something different. They felt, lately, perched on the edge of the next phase in life. The no-baby phase. They were excited, invigorated, planning, lounging, reading *The New Yorker* and *Harper's* uninterrupted while Tom and Mike played happily by themselves. They would look up at each other from their respective magazines, the heartwarming, tinkling sound of the boys playing in their bedroom (they got along so well, for the most part, occasionally fighting over toys, but it was nothing big, nothing constant) drifting in to where they lay on the couch, and husband and wife would rub their toes against one another, smiling. This joy, this newness, this hopefulness for a future, *damn it*, made them swell with love for one another. And, ironically, this new love caused the particular problem Sonia is dealing with right now.

She wipes herself and stands and turns on the light. The evil little stick in her hand has grown a dark, bleeding pink line in the middle of it, as sure as can be. There is no mistaking it. For a fleeting moment she thinks, happily, well at least the hormones are strongly present, nearly ensuring that she won't miscarry. Then, as quickly as the thought occurs to her, the feeling of horror returns. No more babies! No more crying, screaming, up-all-night babies! No more fucking babies!

Sonia places the stick on a high shelf in the bathroom, saving it to show to Dick later that night, when he returns from Denver, where he is away on a business trip. Barefoot, wearing an AC/DC concert T-shirt she's had since the seventh grade, she pads quietly down the stairs from her loft bedroom, picking up a plastic dinosaur as she passes through the living room, and heads straight to the coffee machine in the kitchen. The kitchen is next to the boys' room, and she wants them to keep sleeping. She needs a moment to herself. She needs some coffee first. Moving in an exaggeratedly careful way, she opens the freezer and gets the can of coffee, puts a filter in the coffeemaker, fills the pot with water, all the while eyeing the closed door where her children sleep.

She stopped drinking coffee altogether when she was pregnant with Tom. When she was pregnant with Tom, that first pregnancy, she stopped smoking, drinking booze and coffee, and she quit her job as a bartender in the East Village. And, lastly, painfully, she quit painting because oils and turpentine were potentially harmful to her unborn child and she hated acrylics. She had, indeed, stopped living life as she knew it when she was pregnant with Tom, and turned into a TV-watching, steak-and-ice-cream-eating, bored and terrified ghost of her former self. With Michael, she'd been a little more relaxed, although it never felt like a small thing, carrying a life inside her body, and the responsibility weighed on her during both pregnancies, really. It hadn't been until recently that she felt less burdened, less fearful, that she laughed easily again. Ah, the recent changes. Her libido back, for one.

Dick and she were fucking again, like they did back when they first met, like so many couples fuck when they first meet. Granted, they've had other short-lived sexual bursts in their marriage—during that middle trimester of pregnancy, particularly the first pregnancy, and when the babies were four months old or so, and her breasts were large with milk but her body was otherwise slimmed down again. But then the baby's teeth came in, keeping them up all night, pacing the living room with a crying baby. Then the lack of sleep crept up on Dick and Sonia, and then the fucking went away, far away. Now it was back. And no teeth were coming in. All teeth were in already. Every last goddamn two-year-old molar was in little Mike's mouth. Now, they weren't tired anymore, not tired like they used to be. Now it was her body he's been fucking, not the strange, temporary lushness of her reproducing self. No, Dick, balding, aging, pale-faced Dick, with his freckles and large shoulders, has been reaching for her, for her skinny, long, angular self.

And Sonia loves it. She feels inspired. Sex and painting were always connected for her and now that she's fucking again, now that she's getting seriously fucked again, she wants to paint. Underneath the back terrace, where blue-stone lines the small, sheltered part of their little, Brooklyn yard, Sonia imagines her easel. The raggedy tree that's too big for the yard, the lovely drooping grape vines, littering the yard with purple berries. It would be a lovely place to paint. She'd need a good, sturdy cabinet with high shelves, just in case Mike gets curious. A stool, although she'll stand and move around. She lies in bed at night, her cunt all drippy and her muscles really relaxed from all that pummeling Dick just gave her, and she imagines what she'll paint. What colors she'll start with. How she'll turn the canvas upside down, to mess with herself, to get herself to think. How she'll turn the canvas around and paint on the back of it. How she'll push herself to not do what is expected of her in her art, because all day long she does what is expected of her at home. And while she stays up in the dark thinking these things, Dick snores, delicately, next to her.

Oh, the wild fucking, the loud groans and heavy panting, the skin slapping against each other, "oh yeah, oh yeah," up in their loft bedroom, on a regular basis. Sonia's feet flung over her head, Dick's hand coming down powerfully on her ass, slapping her, "smack," both drunk from three glasses of wine at dinner. They love fucking each other. No, it isn't anything new, fucking the same person for ten years, but that is OK with both of them. And now that they have their energy back, now that they feel emotionally less ruined by the constant demands of babies, now they just want each other, really. After the kids go to sleep, they pour that extra glass of wine, play some Miles Davis, and talk. The comfort of familiarity, mixed with their belief that they can possibly be someone else, be what they really want to be, what they were destined to be before they got sidetracked by the births of their children. Sonia decided to let her hair grow to her shoulders, even though she may be a little old for long hair. Dick grew a small, trim, well-groomed beard.

And now she's pregnant. After being so careful, using condoms or her cervical cap or sometimes both. But no birth control is perfect, except for maybe the pill, which gave her anxiety attacks, so she couldn't really take it.

Curling up with her coffee on the couch in the living room, she looks down from her third-floor walk-up apartment, out the windows and into the back yards and trees of her neighbors. The sun begins to creep up through the green canopy. A certain tension leaves her as she realizes that she had managed to make coffee without waking the kids.

HER SOPHOMORE YEAR of high school, in South Bend, Indiana, where she grew up, she'd had a pretty serious boyfriend, a guy by the name of Bruce Rogers. It was to him she'd lost her virginity. There'd been some sex education then, in the late seventies and early eighties, but mostly she learned from talking with friends. Her best friend Larissa had been having sex with her boyfriend, and boys before that, and talked about it all the time. As a younger girl, a junior high school student, Sonia would curl up in her parent's closets and rifle through her father's *Playboys*. Afterward, she'd pull up her T-shirt, staring at her pink budded nipples in dismay. Would she ever have breasts? She wanted desperately to be desirable. She never grew breasts in junior high, nor high school, really. She hadn't grown a decent pair of breasts until her milk came in, after Tom was born. But, in high school, she learned how to wear padded bras, tight pants, and black eyeliner, and that seemed to work well enough.

Bruce Rogers desired her, more or less. He would fuck

her, gently for the most part, earnestly and quickly, without ever making eye contact. Sonia, staring off to the side while he humped her, was always amazed that someone else's body part was inside her. It felt big. It felt like a big deal. And, truthfully, Bruce liked her. They were "going together." They held hands in public. They made out passionately at football games and at the Taco Bell, licking each other's faces and the insides of each others' mouths with a tongue-thrusting abandon. He thought she was funny and smart and real. They both loved AC/DC, Led Zeppelin, and Van Halen. So when a condom fell off inside of her after fucking in the backseat of his Chevy Chevette one Friday night, Bruce seemed concerned. He wasn't a dick about it, like her friend Larissa's eighth grade boyfriend had been. He didn't stop talking to her, in other words.

At first, when she was late, she didn't worry about it. She wasn't that regular anyway. But then, at the Taco Bell one night, when she was a solid two weeks late, she became very dizzy and threw up her entire dinner. That worried her and she and Bruce discussed it and he knew a doctor on the other side of town who could give her a test and anything else she needed.

Dr. Federshneider was a nice man. His office smelled a little unclean but when Sonia returned to hear the results of the blood test—he wouldn't tell her over the phone— she knew she wanted him to be the one to "take care of things." He smiled at her warmly, with real concern. So what if his hair was dirty? The worst was waiting for "the time to be right," as Dr. Federshneider put it.

"Right now," he said, holding his fingers together to demonstrate, "the cluster of cells are so small, that I could miss some of them and that would cause trouble. You need to be at least six weeks along."

This was not an easy waiting time. It was only another week or so. But her mother seemed to notice that the bathroom garbage wasn't full of pads and discarded tampons. Sonia was throwing up all the time now, not just after eating at Taco Bell. At the dinner table during this time—dinner being a family affair in their household—her mother Marie, who'd been raised Catholic as her Spanish ancestors before her, sermonized on the evils of premarital sex and abortion. Sometimes she talked about other things, but it was pretty normal dinner conversation. She didn't picket abortion clinics, but she did love talking about the evils of it.

Sonia flung herself out of the chair and into the bathroom where she promptly threw up the meatloaf she'd just eaten, bits of onion and ground beef clinging to the inside of her nostrils. Her mother knocked on the door, alarmed, asking, "Are you OK? Sonia, are you OK?"

"I'm fine!" She screamed at her mother. "You just make me sick!"

"Young woman . . ." but Sonia was pushing past her

now, running up into her own room, where she slammed her door shut and turned on her stereo. She had a lock on the inside of her door. Her mother banged and banged for a while, and then gave up.

It was all over soon enough. The Saturday came when she had an appointment. Bruce came with her, but couldn't hold her hand throughout the procedure. It hurt, the vacuuming out of her womb. Drugged and not feeling well, Bruce drove her to Larissa's house where she was conveniently having a sleepover, rubbing her shoulders as they drove.

"Do you think it had a soul?" Sonia asked him.

"I don't know, Sonia. I don't know if anyone has a soul."

That night, they watched TV nonstop, Sonia getting up carefully to go change her pads every hour or so. Larissa's mother was a cocktail waitress, and divorced and never around. Not that she would have cared that Sonia was convalescing at her house, or judged her for having an abortion. Sonia healed quickly. And she never doubted, for a minute, that she'd done the right thing. But doing the right thing wasn't always pleasant or easy. It didn't always make you feel good about yourself.

SONIA HEARS STIRRING IN the boys' room. Quietly, the door opens and there they stand, sleepy and disoriented. Tom with his dirty blonde hair and blue eyes, just like Sonia, even the shape of his face, slightly round and chinny. And Mike, still a baby, but a more mysterious genetic creature, very fair hair and long-faced, reminding Sonia of her father one minute and her husband the next. When they first wake in the morning, her love for them surges through her, warming the top of her head, making her hands feel tingly. They are hers! It's unbelievable! Vulnerable, fresh, a look in their eyes that says: each day is a new universe. For a split second, Sonia feels inspired. What could be more important than taking care of these creatures that came from her womb? What could be more delicious, more pleasurable? They run up to her, both of them, and jump into her lap, rubbing their eyes. Tom, in an effort to throw his arms around his mother's neck, knocks her cup of coffee. Coffee spills on the blue couch, and the caffeine is now what surges in her veins, strong and chemical, erasing all effects of warmth and calm and love, and Sonia says "shit!" pushing Tom off of her, immediately regretting her language—but she can't always control everything, right?—and then, sharply, "Can't you be more careful?"

The moment of bliss, of purpose, is broken. By her own stupidity. Because coffee on the couch is nothing, but being nasty to her four-year-old, a common occurrence, really, feels unforgivable, particularly first thing in the morning. The shame, the guilt, the desire to be away from herself, away from her flawed mothering, is now the current pulling her under. The speed with which her emotions turn upside down. The alarmingly fast exchange of happiness and gratitude for self-disgust and impatience. She tries to right things. "Don't worry, Tom. I'm sorry I yelled. I'll get a towel, it's no big deal."

"Shit is a bad word, mommy."

Sonia ignores him and fetches a towel. Her day has begun. She can't stand it. She can't stand to be in her apartment, the children clawing at her. Out. She needs out.

"Let's go, let's get out of here, let's go to the park," she says, bending over to fruitlessly wipe at the brown stain on the couch. The boys stand, watching her. "We can get ice creams."

"Ice cream!" Tom squeals and starts running randomly—to the TV set, to the kitchen, "Ice cream! Ice cream, yeah, yeah!" Mike, too, starts running in circles, saying, "Ice cream! Ice cream!"

It's not yet eight in the morning and Sonia's already promised them ice cream. What is wrong with her? Is she that desperate? She's pregnant, she remembers, relieved that something besides herself is to blame. That's why she's behaving so badly! She consoles herself with this thought, but really, she often resorts to strange, needy bribes to get through the day.

After sticking them in front of the TV, she showers and dresses. She pulls on the same elastic waist, black-turning-greyish-green cotton pants from the Gap that she wears, quite literally, every day. Her bra has brown stains under the armpits. She fastens it hastily, pulling her loose-skinned, now small again, breasts around a bit to fit them in properly. Her breasts will grow again, as her pregnancy continues, and this excites her. She loves her breasts when she's pregnant, even more when she's nursing.

The phone rings. It's Dick. "Hi, honey. I'm getting on a plane after the meeting this morning. I shouldn't be home too late."

"I'm pregnant."

"What?"

"You heard me, I'm pregnant." Sonia shakes her foot anxiously. She hunches over the phone. "I'm fucking pregnant. I just took a test." There's a pause. "Well, say something, asshole."

"Listen, I'm just a little shocked. Maybe it's a mistake. I mean, we've been really careful . . ."

"It's not a fucking mistake. Fuck you. It's not my fault, either, Dick. What do you mean *we've* been really careful? And someone's not been careful? I'm not fucking anyone else, for your information, and I resent—"

"My god! You are pregnant! I know it! Because you are already being a psychotic cunt!"

Sonia slams the phone down. "Let's go, boys! Let's go get ice cream," she hollers, as she heads down the steps from her loft into the living room, where they sit glued to cartoons. "It's beautiful out! Let's go to the park!"

"Yeah, yeah, ice cream! The park! Yeah!" The boys follow her out the door and down the walk-up steps. She grabs her stroller, shoved in a closet in the entranceway, and she swiftly belts Mike into it. Tom grabs a hold of the stroller and out they go, the three of them, in search of fake milk products glittering with food coloring and a bench in a shady spot at one of the parks, where Sonia will plant her exhausted and already sickly self as her children pretend to be dinosaurs and other ungodly creatures, destroying all that is around them with their special powers.

3

One of the more strategic events of Sonia's days involves picking the right park in the Cobble Hill area of Brooklyn. Her two main concerns are the crowd—who will be there? will it be too crowded?—and in the summer, whether or not there is shade. In the winter, of course, she searches out the sunny spots. But the last thing she needs today is to cook in some hot-as-hell, breeze-free, garbage-can-and-diaper-stink asphalt playground. She opts for Carroll Park, a long walk down Court Street, but worth it for shade and general anonymity. She carries her cell phone, thinking to call a friend, but rarely does. She is a cell phone hater for the most part. The closer parks, the parks on Henry Street built near the Long Island College Hospital, have become for Sonia unbearably full of women who know each other. Incestuous. They're nice playgrounds and she feels lucky to have them just around the corner from her Atlantic Avenue apartment, but socially, they feel like high school. Sonia hated high school, for the most part. She liked her friends, and she liked certain classes, but the in-group, the out-group, the viciousness of it, repelled her. At Carroll Park she occasionally runs into women she knows, but mostly these are women she likes, and more often, there's no one she knows.

Sometimes this is what she wants. Anonymity. No small talk. Or big talk. To be alone in a crowd, or just to be alone. To maybe chat briefly with some mother she doesn't know, but to be able to sit and read, or sit and think, occasionally pushing Mike in the swing or cuddling and tussling her boys before they leap up to run around like the maniacs they are. Because they are maniacs, really. Just like every other boy she knows, and some little girls. Wanting never to sit still, not even at mealtime, thank you, turning everything into a gun: their little fingers, a stick, a carrot, a plastic spoon. (Sonia, on pressure from all the other Brooklyn mothers, doesn't buy toy guns for her kids.) Tom even once pointed a tampon at her he'd fished out of her purse. Sonia loves all this boy energy, the mayhem, the straightforward aggression. Having grown up with one sister, a ladylike little girl who made Sonia feel clutzy and wild, and her domineering mother, she loves having her boys. She loves their lack of passivity, their lack of calculation.

When Sonia arrives at Carroll Park, it's early in the day

yet, and all but empty. The air is still clear and slightly cool and an abundance of shady benches lie outstretched before her. On a far bench, at the end of the playground, is one other person, a friend of Sonia's, a woman named Clara. They wave at one another. Short, mousy hair; big, plain brown eyes; a ski-jump nose; a bow mouth; wearing a collared shirt always, Clara is the most conservative person Sonia knows, in both dress and politics. Right out of a prep-school, field-hockey-uniform catalogue. Living proof that Talbot's still matters greatly to many. Clara runs in marathons, plays tennis (Sonia wants to learn now too), has a beige couch with a matching beige armchair and a beige rug.

And yet, something is off with Clara. Something is deeply off with her, and it is this fucked-upness that Sonia is really drawn to. The outward appearance so controlled, so perfect, flawless, unassailable, and yet Clara is crazy, Sonia knows it—she just doesn't know exactly how crazy, or why. Clara is someone that Sonia is happy to run into today. Her son Sam plays fairly well with Tom, and little Mike will follow the big boys around, content to watch their intricate play scenarios. They won't let Mike play, unless they designate him the pet dog or, as was once the case, the giant rat, but Mike doesn't care, as long as he doesn't get hit or left totally behind. Neither does Sonia. And Clara's daughter, Willa, either sits quietly by their side, playing tea party games by herself or finds another little girl to play with.

They smile and wave and say hello. They don't embrace or even kiss the sides of cheeks. No contact. Clara is not like that. Sonia is flexible, very kiss-cheeky with mothers who like to be kiss-cheeky, and physically distant from those who prefer physical distance. Clara prefers distance. But she's warm and kind and Sonia, despite feeling unwell—her mouth is dry, she's a bit dizzy, could it all be psychological? She couldn't really already be feeling horrible from the pregnancy—feels better in Clara's presence. All that lovely beigeness, the desire for beigeness at least, emanating from her bones. And, frankly, Clara doesn't know her that well. Clara is a new friend. Sonia feels like a blank slate around Clara. She feels she can reinvent herself. She feels hopeful, new, attractive.

But today there is also the question of whether to tell Clara that she's pregnant. Although Sonia loves this new friendship, there is something to be said for knowing someone well before you tell them that you are pregnant and are not sure if you plan to keep the baby. Because Sonia is not sure. She has no idea what to do. There would be comfort in sharing the news of her state, and her ambivalence, with someone like Ginny, a woman who no longer lives in Brooklyn. Ginny, Sonia knows, has had a few unwanted pregnancies. Ginny believes in family planning. And regardless of the liberal posturing of many residents of Cobble Hill, Brooklyn, almost everyone, or so it seems to Sonia, is really ruled by fear and hate. All the allegedly liberal mothers in her neighborhood—with the spiritual Eastern symbol tattoos and Crocs—really think being a mother is *sacred*. Children are sacred, and mothers should take care of them and be sacred, too. She met a Yoga instructor who once said that women with regular jobs deserved to have their children beaten by West Indian nannies because how could they leave their children all day? This, from a Yoga instructor! And then there was the actress, a friend she thought she knew, educated, hip, who had stared at her in disgust when Sonia admitted to having had an abortion and changed the subject immediately to stage acting versus film. No, Sonia could never tell what people were really thinking. And no one's appearance guaranteed anything.

But that's the thing about Clara. She looks so damn conservative. Yet lurking beneath the Izod and penny loafers is a mystery, something beyond conservative or liberal.

The boys run toward each other and then off to the jungle gym. Sonia sits on the bench, glancing down first to check for pigeon shit. A metal handrail separates her from Clara.

"Bill's been out of town for a week now. I'm starting to go nuts," Clara says. "Just a little bit. I mean, I'm fine. Sam and Willa are fine. But I find it hard sometimes when he's gone on big business trips. He normally works late a few nights a week, but just to have him around a couple of nights, you know, and the weekend. I mean, Sam doesn't even give a shit that his dad is gone. Isn't that bad? What's the point of having a father if he's never around?"

"Dick's been in Denver for two days and I can't wait for him to return. It's harder when they're not here, for sure." Sonia knows she's a wimp in comparison to Clara. Dick hardly ever travels for business. Clara's husband Bill is nearly always gone. At least two weeks out of the month. And yet, Clara has never complained to her before. She usually acts so nonchalant about Bill's absences. "Why is this time different? With Bill being gone?"

"It's not that this time is different. No, what I think is happening is that I'm realizing what our home is like. I'm newly aware of certain things, and I don't know why that is. The weather? The beginning of summer? Something is making me see my home clearly and I don't like what I see." Clara looks over at Sam. He's playing listlessly on the jungle gym. Sonia scans for her sons, too. The sun warms her head, and she's feeling at peace for a moment. Sometimes, hearing other people's troubles does this to her, gives her peace with her own shortcomings.

"Sam watches five hours of TV a day. Yesterday, for the first time, I kept track of how many videos I put in and how many times I turned on the cartoons and I counted, I goddamn counted how much TV he watched, and it was five hours. Five fucking hours of television. Now, maybe nothing's wrong with that, but the truth is, he doesn't talk very well for a four-year-old and I can't help but wonder if it's because I tune out and stick him in front of the TV so much. He loves the TV on and I grew up with the TV on and I think I'm normal. But I just wonder if there was someone else around, if I weren't so burnt out all the time, if the TV would maybe be on less. And maybe Sam would talk better. And maybe I'd enjoy this whole motherhood thing more. I love my kids, you know that, but I just find the whole thing so damn hard. Why's it so hard? And what if someone else were around, really around? Now, don't get me wrong, I love Nadine, my babysitter. She's a great babysitter, but she's a babysitter. She's not emotionally invested in my kids. She's not. She cares for them, she takes good care of them, but she's not their parent. It's different. And Willa, bless her, she's so easy on me, but I feel bad as a role model for her. I'm always tired. I sit around, tired. And she sits around me, looking tired, too. Like she's trying to imitate me or something."

Sonia nods. Willa stares at the two of them, her mouth set in a pout. She's two, just like Mike, and yet nothing like Mike. She freaks Sonia out. Whereas with Mike, Sonia feels she can still say whatever she wants to in front of him, because he's still in his little baby world, with Willa, she feels different. She feels spied upon. She feels judged. She feels like this little two-year-old girl is already sizing her up to see how she can bring her down. She feels like Willa knows how to be mean already. Not hitting on impulse, without thinking about it, like her boys do. Not

that kind of meanness, not the behaving without thinking sort of spontaneous behavior. No, Willa, two-year-old
Willa, who's still in diapers, who still sucks on her thumb,
already knows how to be a fucking bitch. She turns her
brown eyes, eyes that look just like her mother's, at Sonia
and asks, "Would you like a cup of tea?"

Sonia hesitates. Could a two-year-old poison tea? Could
she poison *imaginary* tea? Sonia takes her cup, but doesn't
pretend to sip, just holds it in her lap.

Clara says, "Run along, Willa. Go play with the boys.
Mommy will play tea party with you later." And Willa, after
glaring at Sonia, sulks off, twitching her diaper-padded
butt at them as she goes. "See what I mean? I'm so desperate for adult conversation! And I just push them away all
the time. Because they're always here. They always need
me. Not Bill, and not Nadine, but me."

Just then, Tom runs up, crying. "Mommy, mommy, Sam
spit on my head." Mike is close behind his brother, very
curious. Sam hides underneath the jungle gym, in a shady
spot. Indeed, there is a large gob of yellow snot on Tom's
head. Sonia can handle this. Frankly, she can handle her
children getting picked on very easily. In fact, she finds it
comforting. As long as they're not being the troublemak-
ers, she can shift into good parent mode. "Just use your
words, Tommy. Tell Sam you don't appreciate him doing
that."

Clara turns red. With rage, or embarrassment, or both,

Sonia is unsure. She runs after her son, grabbing him from beneath the jungle gym with her buffed-up, marathon-running body and drags him by his shirt collar to the bench. "YOU APOLOGIZE TO TOM RIGHT NOW. YOU HEAR ME? NEVER, EVER, DO I WANT TO HEAR THAT YOU'VE SPIT ON ANOTHER KID. TOM IS YOUR FRIEND, SAM, AND YOU'RE LUCKY TO HAVE HIM WITH THE WAY YOU BEHAVE. WHAT IS WRONG WITH YOU?" She pulls his little face up to hers, her hand grasping his chin roughly.

"I'm sorry, Tom, I'm sorry!" Sam weeps and holds on to his neck, from where the collar of his shirt scraped him. His chin is red where his mother roughed him up. He runs back under the jungle gym and cries, face in hands.

"Clara, don't worry about it," Sonia says, a little freaked out. But, also, this outburst, this complete failure to behave reasonably, is what Sonia loves about Clara. She kind of sucks, she really does. She loves her children, but she loses her shit all the time. Often, she's so damn vulnerable, so *not* superior and smug like many of the parents Sonia knows. Not that Sonia enjoys watching Clara's children suffer when she freaks out, no. The suffering pains her. But against her better self, she appreciates watching Clara fuck up. The mystery that is Clara, the flawlessly preppy clothes, the house on the right block in the best part of Cobble Hill, a thin gold wedding band her only adornment. All that outward modesty, togetherness, rightness, calmness, all of it seems so desperate. God knows what is hiding beneath it. It's always been Sonia's theory, from experience, that the most normal looking people are completely bonkers. Sonia wipes the top of Tom's head with a wet wipe from her stroller bag and gives Mike, who stands there confused and intrigued, a kiss on the head and pats them both on the behind. "We have thirty minutes more of playtime, then we need to run errands."

Clara breathes out heavily. "I just don't know what to do, Sonia. I'm so sorry about Sam spitting on Tom, I am. He loves Tom. Tom is one of his only friends. He is always so happy to see him. You saw him run up to Tom when you guys got here."

"Don't worry about it, Clara. My kids aren't perfect. No kids are perfect. They all do weird shit sometimes."

"But I am really worried about Sam. I am. He's so angry lately and I can't help but think it's because Bill's not around enough. On the one hand, he's fine, he doesn't miss his father. And when his father is around, he doesn't really care. Because they don't know each other, or rely on each other. But it's as if Sam knows something is missing, even though he doesn't know what. And it makes him angry. And I just wonder if I were a little more patient with Sam, if he wouldn't be so angry."

"Hey, Clara." Sonia gets up. "You want to corral the kids and go get an ice cream? Sometimes it's good to just walk down the street a bit, get out of the park."

Clara looks up, looks distracted. The mothers go through the ordeal of getting the children, which isn't so difficult when ice cream is involved. They exit, carefully closing the park door behind them, and head down to Court Street.

Clara continues on as they maneuver their strollers through busy sidewalks. "Don't get me wrong, I love the money Bill makes," she says. "And, I'll be honest with you, he makes a lot of money. And that is very important to me. We get the great ski vacations. I shop a lot and I love to shop. Soon, we'll buy a house in Connecticut. I really, really want that house in Greenwich. Not sort of or kind of, no—" and here Clara throws her arms up, "I really, really want that house. And if it weren't for Bill working like he does, that house wouldn't be a possibility. It's just sometimes I feel no different than some ghetto, single mother raising her kids. Yes, I can afford help. But the help, the immigrant women I hire, are from the ghetto, essentially. And like I said, I love Nadine. I got a real good one this time. She's a good, caring woman, and that's not always the case, you know. And yet I feed the kids noodles five nights a week, they watch TV nonstop, our house is full of cheap plastic toys they ignore, and they don't know their own father. So what is the difference between me and some single mother from the housing projects? Tell me? Sam watches Pokémon just like them. And he eats the same shit they eat. And they hang out with burnt-out women day and night. Tell me, am I different? I love that he makes a lot of money. But he's not around, you know?"

"Maybe you need a vacation, Clara. Some time to yourself. Next time Bill comes back, go away for a weekend alone."

Clara looks shocked. "I'd never leave my kids overnight. I just couldn't do that."

And here is where Sonia wants to yell at her, to shake her muscled shoulders and say, "But you're being mean to your kids! You are around them too much and you're being mean to them and that's not OK! Leaving them to gain your sanity might be the best thing for them!"

But instead she says, "Clara, I'm pregnant. And I don't know what to do."

4

When Sonia arrives, Clara sets the table for two and moves back to the stove where she's cooking rice. The top of the pan pops around nicely, steam barely escaping, the smell of salt and grain and butter rising, a comforting smell for Sonia's still delicate nature. For the kids, Clara made a big vat of macaroni and cheese. Paper plates and plastic cups sit on a lower table, a kid's table, in the living room in front of the TV. Sonia watches her as she then gets out a chopping board and dices ginger, sweet onion, and oranges and strawberries.

"I'm making a chutney for the red snapper," she explains to Sonia and Sonia thinks, *oh no, not fish*, but says nothing.

Clara's kids are upstairs in the bath. She left the door open, so she can hear what's going on. Sam makes boat noises. She can't hear Willa.

She screams in the direction of the bathroom, "WILLA?

ARE YOU OK? DARLING? ANSWER ME!"

There's no answer. Again she screams, "SAM? SAM? IS YOUR SISTER OK UP THERE?"

The boat noises stop. Sam says, "Willa's fine, mommy. She's just sitting here. She's got her finger up her nose."

"YOU SCREAM DOWN TO ME HERE IF WILLA GOES UNDER WATER OR SOMETHING. YOU HEAR ME, SAM?"

"OK!"

Sonia asks, "Do you want me to go check on them?"

"Oh no, I'm sure they're fine." Clara gives her the once over that Clara sometimes gives her, examining her quickly, but very closely. This makes Sonia uncomfortable, but it's always a brief thing, and then Clara is back to being Clara—loud, self-absorbed even when talking about other people or her children. But she's got a heart. Sonia knows this, appreciates this. Because not everyone has a heart. And it wasn't as if Sonia didn't notice things about Clara.

ONCE, WHEN THE TWO were coming back from a movie in a cab—they'd managed to get their husbands to watch the kids on a Sunday night so they could go see *Girl, Interrupted*—Sonia felt so much taller than Clara. She felt like Clara was a little girl, really. And then, as soon as they got out of the cab, they were the same height again. This strange confusion of bodies, the same size but for the opposite reason, as Clara is all legs. Clara, resembling an ostrich, or really, some kind of fast African plains animal. Something that's built to run. And Clara is built to run. She ran marathons while Sonia got winded chasing her sons. Clara had played field hockey in high school while Sonia was smoking weed and having sex. Sonia's endorphin highs came from drugs and getting laid while Clara's came from running for as long as she could, as fast as possible. The altered state, the endorphins, the just breathing, just moving, of running marathons. The idea of it, the sheer mindlessness of it boggled Sonia. Clara runs every marathon she can get to, even now, with the two kids. When Nadine comes to watch the kids, she goes running. And she long ago gave up the idea of a career, despite her master's degree in health administration. Sonia wishes she could be so content. She even thinks maybe Clara will rub off on her.

Clara's husband Bill is away again, after being home for only three days and nights, where he spent all of one night at home, trying to keep the kids off of him so he could read the paper and watch a game on TV at the same time, according to Clara. And Sonia believes it. She's grateful Bill is not there—he is not Sonia's favorite person. In fact, she actively dislikes him. He doesn't flirt. And he's just a garden variety dick of a man. Never smiles. He may even be dumb, Sonia theorizes, regardless of his good career. And it was clear that regardless of how much Clara complained of the difficulty of being alone with the kids so

much, Clara didn't mind his many absences, nor his tenu-
ous relationship to his own children. Clara often made it
clear that having him around was harder than not. One
more person in her house to pick up after.

Sonia brings a bottle of wine out of her bag as her sons
go off into the living room where the TV is already on.

"Oh, you didn't need to bring anything!" Clara says,
taking the bottle.

"I so appreciate you inviting us over. I've been so
exhausted lately. And you didn't have to cook for us. We
could have ordered pizza . . . "

"Let me get my kids out of the bath." Clara runs upstairs,
shouting—"Tom and Mike are here, you guys! And you all
get to watch a video!"—then she's back in the kitchen.

Sonia watches Clara's back as she aggressively chops
things and remembers the day at the park, not so long
ago, three weeks maybe?, when she told her. And then,
when she started to cry, and when she told her how Dick
had reacted! Calling her a cunt. When Sonia said the
word, quietly then, because other mothers had started to
come to the park—alone together they swore like sailors
as long as the kids seemed out of earshot—the way Clara
looked at her as she said the word "cunt." It was as if she
had said something to turn Clara on, as if Clara's face
turned lascivious upon hearing the word "cunt." Sonia
had wanted Clara to be enraged for her, with her, and
instead, she went all glassy eyed and her mouth hung

open. And then she snapped out of it. Back to where
Sonia needed her.

Clara puts in a two-hour movie, not too scary for the
little ones, not too boring for the big ones.

Sonia, in the kitchen, opens the bottle of wine she
brought. "Would you like a glass? I hope you don't mind I
just got started while you were getting the video on."

"I'd love a glass!"

"Cheers," they say at the same time, laughing at that, the
synchronicity of it, and they clink their glasses together.

"Here's to husbands at work!" Clara says. She adds,
"May they stay there forever!" Sonia, her mouth already
around the rim of her glass, smiles at her with her eyes.

"I know I'm not supposed to drink, but I'm only going
to have one glass."

"In France they'd be forcing you to drink! Don't even
think about it!"

Sonia sits down at the table. She knows she doesn't
look well. She looks pregnant. Greenish complexion,
saggy cheeks, dark circles around the eyes. She looks like
something inside of her is stopping her from focusing
outward. Clara starts chopping asparagus. The rice bubbles, providing the only sound for a minute. Sonia says,
"Yeah, husbands at work forever. Not a bad thought.
Actually, I feel bad about how I complained about Dick
the other day . . ."

"Don't feel bad! I was complaining about Bill. We live

with these bastards! What else are we supposed to do but complain about them?"

"No, I know, it's hard to live with people, anyone really. By the end of each year of college, I truly hated my room-mates. After living together for a year, our friendship would end. Living with people made me hate them. Still does, really. It's just hard, no matter how much you love a person, to live with them. And for eight years? Fifty years? I just don't know how people do it. It seems so unnatural."

"Well, that's why I say, here's to husbands away at work!"

"But anyway, that night, when Bill came home from Denver, we had a really good talk. And he apologized for yelling at me. I just don't want you to think my husband is a complete asshole."

"Ah, they always say they're sorry, but are they really sorry? Are they? They say they're sorry because they just want to get us off their backs."

Sonia laughs weakly. "There's some truth to that, undoubtedly. But I think he felt real remorse. Work has been really tough on him lately. With the launch of a new business model, brought on by these new partners in his research firm. And he was just shocked that I could be pregnant. Really shocked. And I was too, as you know. It's hard news to handle. It's hard news to believe, really.

"So we talked about it. About how I don't know what to do. And we talked about whether we could afford three kids and the answer to that is, we could, if we go with public schools. As long as we don't attempt the private school thing, which is OK with me, I guess. I don't know. And we talked about our apartment and whether or not we would have to move. And that's a possibility. If it's a girl, eventually we would need to move. I guess three boys could share that one bedroom. It is big enough. I don't know. Maybe I should look into the suburbs. Or Kensington. Have you heard of Kensington? Further out on the F train, in Brooklyn? Past Park Slope? I hear it's got good schools and we could afford a house there. It's not here though, it's not Cobble Hill. It's not nearly as . . . sophisticated. It's much more middle class."

Clara pours herself another glass of wine but says nothing and yet Sonia knows what she is thinking. Public schools? Not in Clara's life. Kensington? Fucking Kensington? She's headed toward Greenwich. Sonia knows that. But she goes on.

"But then there's the fact that we just don't want, I mean, we always planned for just two, and it's not too late to do something about it, although it's getting there. I would have to do something right away. And my painting. And maybe if we got more help I could paint and take care of three kids. But he's just being very supportive of whatever I decide to do. And giving me time and space. And getting up with the boys in the mornings before he goes to work, because I'm not feeling well. He knows I'm the one who'll be doing most of the childcare, so he really is deferring to me regarding the final decision. But I look at this man, you know, I look at my husband and I think, could he respect me, would he feel the same way about me, his wife, if I aborted his baby?"

"It's not a baby yet, Sonia. I mean, I understand what you're saying and I would be supportive of whatever you do. Having a baby, or not having a baby. And I would never, ever tell a soul if you decided to not keep it," Clara says, "But you would be aborting a fetus, not a baby. A fetus in the first trimester of growth. I miscarried! Twice! Does that make me a criminal? Or just because it was an accident, instead of premeditated, that makes it OK? Involuntary manslaughter in comparison to first degree murder? I mean, what are we talking about here?"

Clara's facial expression reminds Sonia of a district attorney on some legal television drama, arguing a case. Professional in her mannerisms—she's not hysterical, her eyes don't exactly bulge—but she's all passion and righteousness.

"My mother was a Catholic, you know. I still can't shake a lot of that Christian shit. I'm haunted by it. But I know, also, that if I choose to have this baby, I have to be happy with my choice. That it's up to me. It's not God's will. It's up to me. Women ruined their lives to bring me this choice and I have no one to blame. I have no way of playing the victim, you know."

"Don't be so hard on yourself, Sonia. It's a tough decision either way. We're not talking about what color to paint the bathroom here. We're talking about another kid. Or not." Clara polishes off her glass of wine and asks, "Would you like some more wine?"

"Just a tiny splash," says Sonia. "I better figure it out soon, though. Cut back on the wine if I decide to keep it." She grins now at Clara, positively grins at her, with nothing short of mischief in her eyes.

"Well, as you know, I studied health admin and you really need to drink a lot to cause any damage. I mean, being pregnant is hard, and a little booze helps you feel better. It's good for you!"

"I should move to France where it's OK to drink a bit when pregnant. But you see, that's the thing. I feel like if I decide to keep the baby, then all these possibilities go away. Moving to Europe, to be closer to my mother, too, since she moved back to Spain. We talked about Europe, how good it would be for the kids. And we talked about my painting. I feel like it's unfair to my kids if I don't make time for what I want. My mother never made enough time for herself and later, blaming us for her misery and failure, and boredom, her lack of life, I remember just thinking, *I didn't ask to be born! I didn't make any demands on her!* But of course, now having children, I realize there are demands made. Sort of. But I don't want my children to be my scapegoats. I don't want that."

"Tell me," says Clara, dishing out the red snapper, the chutney, the perfectly cooked rice, the tender stalks of asparagus, "you say Dick might not respect you if you decide to abort. But have you expressed that fear to him? Do you think he really wants you to keep it?"

"This looks amazing, Clara. I haven't been feeling that great. But this looks so great." Sonia feels a queasiness upon her but is determined to hide it. Is it the wine? Sonia's stomach is probably a mess. She's pregnant. She's in that first trimester when the smell of food makes you want to vomit. She tentatively picks at the fish. She is going to force herself to eat it and she already knows what the result of that will be. "I think he wants me to keep the baby. I think he's hoping this one will be a girl. I think he wants a daughter." At this thought, Sonia relaxes, smiles at Clara, who again seems to be giving her one of those slack-faced looks, drunkenly so, and she shoves an enormous piece of fish in her mouth.

5

Later that night, after the kids fall asleep without a bath—but who cares, they get one almost every night—after she shuts off the lights in the kitchen and bags the garbage which stinks to high hell—maybe that's what did it, the garbage—Sonia throws up red snapper and chutney in her bedroom bathroom. She only drank one glass of wine, it couldn't be that. No, it's because she's fucking pregnant. Her body tries again, but nothing comes out, and now it's the dry heaves. Again. And again. Fuck. And it was so nice of Clara to cook for her. So nice to see Clara, and this time, no problems with the kids. The kids were great, albeit stoned in front of some crazy Disney movie. And Clara, so sympathetic, really. She drank the rest of the bottle of wine and then opened the next and Sonia was a little surprised, but not really. Because Clara's weird wild streak hiding under her pageboy haircut and navy blue Izod always reared itself. In some way or another. And Sonia likes to think of her as the friend with whom she could go see a band, the friend with whom she could go to a bar. Of course, Bill is never around so Clara can't leave at night, unless she hires Nadine to work late. And what's wrong with Sonia anyway, wanting to go out to bars at night? A married woman? Why would she want to do that?

Because she does. Because she just fucking does. She misses bars. She loved bartending. It was something, besides painting, that she was good at.

Sonia rinses her mouth, but is afraid to use toothpaste, the thought of minty bubbles making her want to dry heave some more. She rinses and rinses and tries to get the fish taste out of her mouth. She can't. Why didn't she say no? Why didn't she say, I'm pregnant and I can't eat this fish? I'll just have some mac and cheese with the kids. She wants to please Clara, that's why. As Clara wants to please her. Ice cream is the answer. Sickly, exhausted, Sonia heads downstairs and quietly—she doesn't want to wake the boys—removes a pint of ice cream from the freezer. Cookie dough ice cream. Afraid even to turn on the lights, she goes into the living room with the pint of ice cream and there in the dark, stuffs her mouth. First slowly, then quickly. And then she sits there, the wet cardboard pint melting in her arm, her eyes off into the dark.

Did Clara try to kiss her? When the movie was over and

they gave the kids Oreo cookies and then she got her stuff: the diaper bag, the Spider-Man action figure that Tom brought over to show Sam, and the stroller out on the sidewalk (the sun was really going down), did Clara, who doesn't do the air-kissy thing and never sits too close—did Clara try to kiss her? The strange lunge, the face next to hers, those big brown eyes, Sonia felt a little woozy from the wine, but it's possible that Clara was full-on drunk. What was that? Was it a pass?

And then, the door opens. In comes Dick. Quietly, as he knows the kids are asleep. He's home so late. It's nine thirty. He looks ruined and Sonia feels very sorry for him. This job, sometimes, seems as if it's sucking his very soul out. It seems like he goes to an office where they stick a vacuum cleaner on his chest and turn it on, without any nozzle, no, just the round metal pole, one of those kind of vacuum cleaners, where the body of it is attached to a long tubular thing, and they put it in right where his heart and soul is and suck out his very life essence. Wordlessly, he sits next to her. He smells like the stale stink of dry, office sweat. The sweat of fear and horror. A different smell than the ripe, wet stink he gets after playing basketball. Not nearly as pleasant. Not pleasant at all actually, whereas sometimes, after basketball on Sundays, they'd put the kids in front of the TV and go upstairs and fuck, quickly and quietly, because Sonia likes that kind of sweat, the liquidy, tangy sweat of his body out in the sun, running around. Yes, that sweat she loves, but this one, this office-hell, are-they-gonna-fire-me, do-I-suck, God-I-hate-my-job sweat, no, this sort of body odor burns her nostrils, especially now that she's pregnant. She moves down the couch a little away from him. He puts his head in his hands.

"Why are you moving away from me? Why would you do that to me? Is it because I'm late? I called to tell you I'd be late. Please don't hate me tonight. I just can't take it."

"No, sweetie, I don't hate you. I'm not mad at you, honestly." She reaches out to him, stretching her arm out, because she doesn't want to get too near to him. He really, really stinks. It must have been an awful day and night at that office. "It's just that you smell bad, honey. And you know how it is when I'm pregnant."

"I smell bad? I SMELL bad?"

"Do you want some ice cream? I threw up the dinner Clara made me. And then I couldn't even brush my teeth because the toothpaste was going to make me vomit. So I couldn't get the fish taste out of my mouth and I'd been dry heaving and I thought ice cream might do the trick. Get rid of the fish flavor, the vomit flavor. Not be minty and bubbly."

"I SMELL bad?"

"Keep your voice down, Dick. The kids are sleeping. What do you want me to say? You want me to lie to you? I'll lie to you from now on and not tell you that you stink when you do. OK? From now on. But I'm pregnant, so just cut me a break. My sense of smell is hyperacute and everything makes me want to vomit. And you know sometimes when you've had a bad day at the office you get a little funky smelling."

"I had a bad day at the office."

"Do you want to talk about it?"

"No." Dick crumples into the couch. The day won. The day clearly defeated him. His eyes are watering, probably from staring at a computer all day, but Sonia is worried he might cry. He rubs them, then puts one of his hands down his pants and audibly scratches his balls.

Sonia, despite her not being able to get too close to Dick, because he stinks like an acidic pile of roach feces, loves her husband just then. His strong bones. His wide shoulders. The fact that the man has a real job. That he is adult enough, responsible enough to have a real job. All of the ones before him sucked with money, pissed money away like it was nothing. And then there was Dick. Quiet, not boring her with his work stuff. So emotionally strong, so dependable. Sometimes he talked to her about work, and it interested her some, it did, but he didn't always talk about work. He wasn't a bore, like some other husbands she knew. His research firm was the best of its kind and Dick's strange, photographic memory made him brilliant at his job. He knew everything he ever looked at. Just stored it all in the vast computer that was his brain. Stinking, or not stinking, she loves this man. And she's sad he's down. She feels for him. She doesn't want him to have bad days.

"Well, if you want to talk about it, I'm here. Ice Cream?"

"No, thanks." He looks at her, his eyes filled with something bad—despair? fear? anger? Dependable, yes, brilliant yes, but inscrutable. And he knows it. And nothing is given away. "You didn't call the doctor or anything, did you?"

"What do you mean?"

"I mean, you're going through with the pregnancy, right?"

"I was just talking about it with Clara."

"And?"

"You know, I thought you wanted me to keep this baby and now I'm trying to figure out your expression and I'm getting the feeling that you don't want me to keep this baby."

"I thought this was about what you want, Sonia."

"Fuck you, Dick. I care what you think. I know it's up to me, but I need to know where you stand."

"You know what I think? You really want to know what I think? That, if you decide to keep this baby, I won't be sure why. That's what I'm thinking right now, that's what I was thinking all day, while I dealt with stupid assholes all day long who frankly, I would never like to talk to again. But I have to. Because we have a family to support, and a growing one at that. And I'm wondering, do we think the world needs our third baby? Do we? Because the world does not need our third baby. Do we think Tom and Mike need less attention than they get? Because I think they get a lot of attention, and I'm not sure anything is wrong with that. And if we know the world doesn't need our third baby and our sons don't need another sibling, then that means we're having this baby because we want another baby! Do we? Is that true? I'm just confused about it. Because I thought we always only wanted two kids."

"Yeah, and then we had an accident. Your fault just as much as mine."

"I know that. You know I know that."

"You want me to get an abortion."

"I just want us to think about it all the way through. I want you to think about what another year of pregnancy means, another year of breastfeeding, another year of a toddler, three more years of diapers. Is that what you want? What about painting? What about that easel in the backyard?"

"You fucking prick."

"What?"

"My mother is Catholic, and—"

"You don't give a shit what your mother thinks. You never have."

"That's not entirely true." But it was mostly true. "Listen, I'll get some babysitting. I will paint. And why do you give a shit if I paint or not? I've never heard you say anything about my painting. And what confuses me more, is I really thought you wanted this. Wanted one more. Then you're going to get that operation, right?"

"Yeah, I'm getting fixed. Don't worry about that. I'm sorry, I just had a bad day. I just had a day where I fantasized I get to quit my job and we can move to Maine and, I don't know, open a bed and breakfast."

"That is a pile of horseshit. You? You can't even fix a chain on a toilet. You suck around the house. Why do you care if I paint, really?"

"Because I want you to be happy?"

"Wrong. You're lying."

And now Dick sighs and lifts his arms over his head stretching his long, monkey-like limbs up toward the high ceiling, and the stale scent that comes from his armpits makes Sonia burp, then gag. "Because I liked you when you painted. I thought you were sexy when you painted. It was something I liked about you."

"Ahhh. And wiping Mike's butt after he's pooped in his diapers is not sexy? Picking a hard green booger out of Tom's nose before preschool, that's not sexy? Cleaning the wax out of their ears after I give them a bath? That doesn't make you hot for me? Playing train, making train noises for my boys, that's not sexy? How about when I pretend I'm batgirl? Come on, that's kind of sexy . . . "

"Maybe if you got that outfit. Black leather. No, wait, that's Catwoman," he says. "I just want to have this baby for the right reasons. That's all. You always wanted it all, you know. I love that about you."

"I still want it all. But I'm not going to have a baby if you don't want another one. Or if you're afraid about the money. And the whole painting thing—here's the deal. If I paint or not, that's my fucking business. Not yours. I don't hold you responsible for my choices."

"Are you sure about that?"

"Yes, I'm sure. And there's no right reason to have a baby. What would be the right reason to have a kid? The world is overpopulated, children are little torture machines, and the planet is dying. So? You fucked me, I accidentally got pregnant. There's only throwing caution to the wind. I can have it all. Tell me, Dick, do you want another kid? Do you want me to have an abortion?"

"I don't want you to have to have an abortion. Especially if you don't want one. I'm just nervous, that's all."

"Well, so am I."

"I love our kids. I'd love our new kid."

"Yeah."

"Don't do anything out of guilt or obligation, Sonia."

"You know me better than that. Now I have to go throw up again. And then, I'm going to bed. Oh, and I think Clara tried to stick her tongue down my throat tonight."

WHY, WHY DOES SONIA decide to keep this baby? Why doesn't she just get an abortion? Catholic guilt? The pleasure she gets from her children is real, but so is the pain, so is the boredom. *Sesame Street?* Wiping butts? Sure, it's a part of life, but is it satisfaction? Is it all she wants? Isn't it fucking boring? Taking care of small children— and nothing else? She has no gift for playground gossip. She gave that occupation up a long time ago. Where's her community? What does she want? She knows she doesn't want to make home decoration her future. She knows she'll never teach elementary school. Or teach anything, for that matter. Can't she be Karen Finley, shoving yams up her ass (Karen's got kids now!) and then smearing it on the canvas? Can't she find a role model that works?

What about that blossoming she felt, that new free- dom, the no-babies feeling? The break she felt was her due? And what about painting? Can't she paint and take care of babies? Can't she paint while she's pregnant? Why this choice and not another? Sonia is convinced there's no right or wrong choice, just a choice to be made, and hers for the making. And why not one more? Three isn't five. It isn't eight. It's three. And then they'll fix their parts like the stray animals they are.

In the meantime, there's life on a daily basis. And a bored woman with half a mind is a dangerous thing.

WHO COULD BE HER role models? It was one thing to rebel against the world as a young childless woman. The tattoo on her ass. The fuck whoever she wants. The safety pins in her ears when she was fifteen. The snarl, the fuck-you middle finger up at the slightest provocation. The anti-cheerleader, anti-good girl.

And yet, of course, there was ambition. But who could be her role models as a mother and a human being in the world, an artist in the world? Georgia O'Keefe? No kids. Frida Kahlo? No kids. Mary Cassatt? Well, not to her taste. The work of women with live-in help, the work of a certain class of women who weren't expected to take care of their children on a daily basis. They could have kids and hire someone else to take care of them day and night and still be considered a good mother. Maybe Sonia was born too late. But that's where all Cassatt's pink comes in. All those mushy brushstrokes, all that pure love. Real love is never pure. Vanessa Bell? Well, maybe if she weren't less important than her childless sister. But then, not even. Sue Coe? Too straightforward, plus, who knows if she has kids?

She wants to be Egon Schiele. She wants to be a man. She wanted to be her instructor, Philbert Rush, not just fuck him, although she only managed the latter. She wants to be a man in her art, for some reason. She doesn't want to represent goodness and motherhood in her art, because that is not all she is, and how often do the two even go together?

And the poets? Adrienne Rich? Angry lesbian poet whose children felt God knows what about her? Yeah, that's right, having a life means torturing your kids. Because even the little punk rock girls with their shocking pink hair who abuse drugs and fuck without condoms still want mommy to give them lots of money, still want mommy to take care of them and, most importantly, still blame their mommies for not loving them enough, or loving them in the wrong way. And, it's probably true. Mothers fuck up their kids. Tough boys, dark boys, art boys, radical boys, listening to Radiohead and heavy metal, fuck, they'd *still* let their mothers wipe the very shit from their assholes if they could, bend over and expose their raw bottoms up, defenseless and needy. Everybody wants a warm meal prepared and served with a smile. Everybody wants to get into a warm bed at night, get tucked into fresh sheets in a dark room. Everybody wants and wants, and nobody says, "That's enough! I'm ready to not be treated warmly, to not get any affection, to not be taken care of!" Fuck, if it's not paying some new age depressive to put cucumbers on your face, it's the next thing. Our needs are endless.

Role models from the poets? Sylvia Plath. Anne Sexton. Crazy stupid bitches who totally screwed up their children. Hey, they were mentally ill! No one would give a shit about their art if they hadn't killed themselves. And what if you love life? What if you have no desire to kill yourself? What if you'd rather kill them instead? Or kill no one, 'cause face it, it's not like Sonia is crazy. She just wants it all.

And who, really, truly, honestly, wants to grow up and become their own mother? Everyone wants a mother, but who wants to be their own mother? No, we're supposed to be learning from their mistakes. Have kids and no life? Study sewing? No, thanks. Be a corporate lawyer, adopt one kid when you turn forty-five, and by that time, you're too fucking old to take care of the poor thing? No, thanks.

And then there are the childless women who for some reason Sonia despises as well. The whiney, self-absorbed ones who remain perpetual children. Who still fucking blame it all on their mothers. Who have no idea. Who reads Virginia Woolf without smelling her forever-a-maiden status? Interior dialogue? Sounds great, if you don't have kids, which thankfully keeps you from such self-absorption. Sonia'd rather read the worst of twice-divorced Jane Smiley with her four kids. At least she has a clue. At least she doesn't have to pretend that art is separate from life. Musicians? Stevie Nicks, Aimee Mann. Past forty years old, clinging to the girl/woman thing. And why not?

Because women are not girls. Their faces sag. Their tits sag. They can't blame it all on being female anymore. They know better because they've been there. Yes, Sonia wanted to be there. And she is there. She just didn't know it would be so hard. All her life, all of her thirty-five years, she's only wanted to experience everything, except maybe heroin addiction. Who are you going to blame now for the mess you're in?

And what if she maybe doesn't want to paint? What if being a housewife is easier in some way? Not trying? Not figuring out if she's as good as they all said she was, so long ago? What if she doesn't want to know if she still knows how to paint? Grandma Moses? Not her plan. But what is her plan? Is she . . . afraid? Afraid she's not all that?

It's true that when Sonia was a little girl, five, six, seven, she wanted to be a boy. They didn't get yelled at as ferociously for jumping all over the furniture. They were supposed to do that. They were boys. If they hit someone, well, it wasn't OK but, hey, what do you expect, they were boys. A five-year-old boy could walk into a room and command more attention, more freedom, absorb more fucking oxygen, than Sonia could at the same age. And she knew it then. But later, well, later, she decided it was fun being female. That being female didn't mean being passive. Thanks to Katrina Nelson. Thanks to the women's movement in the sixties and seventies. Thanks to a lot of people and things, but, really, thanks to Katrina, the friend that changed her life, the friend she met while waiting on tables, the nineteen-year-old high-school dropout from Kalamazoo, Michigan, who changed her life when they met in Boston. Maybe there are no role models. Maybe there are just people, and some more influential than others.

Last she heard, Katrina had married and had a baby, was still living in the Boston area. Maybe Sonia should go visit her.

But Sonia's having this baby.

The decision's been made.

"Do you have to kill a cow to get meat?" Tom asks Sonia this as they walk slowly down Court Street. Mike is asleep in the stroller, his hair dark with sweat and plastered to his red face. It is hot. It is August in Brooklyn. The air is so thick, so humid, that Sonia can't see very well what's in front of her.

"Yes, you have to kill a cow to get meat, sweetheart."

"Does everyone have meat inside of them? Do bugs have meat inside of them? Do I have meat inside of me?"

"Well, yes, I guess so. But we don't eat bugs or people. We eat fish, cows, chickens. Pigs."

"I love meat. Can we get some meat? Can we have hamburgers for dinner tonight?"

Tom starts rubbing his chest. He, too, is red-faced. Sonia's heart constricts, and for a moment, she fears that her children will die from the heat. That their red little faces mean they are dying.

"Sure, let's go pick up some groceries and then go home. It's so hot out here. I think we'd be better off inside, with the air conditioning going. Are you OK, Tom? You look so hot."

"I am hot! I am hot meat!"

This comment makes Sonia dizzy. "Let's go get the groceries and get indoors. I can't take this heat." They walk by a group of construction men digging up a hole in the street. A jackhammer screams in their ears. Cement dust burns their eyes—Tom starts coughing and Sonia's eyes tear. They run to get by the mess. Every corner, it seems, is being dug up. For what, thinks Sonia? New pipes? How can every corner in Brooklyn need new pipes every summer? It feels like a lie. Like a conspiracy to torture mothers into moving to the suburbs.

"Mommy, when I'm five years old, I'll be a big boy, right?"

"Yes, love, but you have quite a ways to go before you turn five. You just turned four a couple months ago."

"I just keep getting bigger! Someday I'll be a grownup, right? And a teenager?"

"Oh heavens, let's not think about it. You're still my little boy. I like you that way."

"But, mom, there's nothing you can do about it." He's smiling now, so excited. And Sonia thinks, *yes, there is*

nothing I can do about it. We all get older, and then we die.
Tom is jumping with excitement. "I'm just going to keep
getting bigger and bigger! And stronger!"

"I know, but I love you just the way you are."

Is he saying this to torture Sonia? Why this obsession
with getting older? And yet, Sonia remembers wanting to
get older, too. When does that change? And what's up with
the whole meat inside of him thing? Sonia can't take it right
now. She hauls the stroller, heavy with Mike, up the three
stairs to the butcher on Court Street. This nearly makes
her cry. Why, why must she be doing this? Why can't she
just do nothing? Why in God's name is she out in this heat
wave, hauling strollers with big sleeping toddlers in them?
Inside, although it is air-conditioned and this feels very
good, the smell of dead animals overwhelms her. Can't she
just feed her kids noodles for the next three months? Forever? Cold air, cold air. Take a breath. There are five other
people there. This seems unbearable to Sonia. How long
will she have to wait to order ground beef? Everyone is at
the butcher's. Everyone is eating meat.

Tom says, "Mom, when I'm ten years old, how old will
you be?"

"I'll be forty, I think."

"Wow! That's really old. Mom, when I'm eleven years
old, how old will Mike be?"

"He'll be nine. Or eight. I can't think right now, Tom.
I'm trying to get us hamburger."

"I'll always be older than Mike, right Mom?"

"Yes."

"And I'll always have more meat inside of me, then. Right?"

"Well, I'm not sure about that." *Help! Help me*, thinks Sonia, as she tries to make eye contact with someone. Is it her turn? Who's been helped? Who's still waiting for help? Sonia has no ability whatsoever to cut a line. Not anywhere, but especially not here, somewhere she goes so often. She looks around, her eyes filled with panic. Who's next? Is she next? Oh, God, she'll never get hamburger. Never.

"Have you been helped?"

Is he talking to her?

"Me?" Sonia asks, pointing her own finger—her whole hand, in fact—at her heaving chest. Her shoulders slope downward and in. Her shoulders nearly shiver with the overwhelmitude of it all. "Am I next?" Her voice is a whisper, which prompts a very loud response from the nice Italian man behind the counter.

"Yes, ma'am!"

"Can I get a pound of hamburger meat? No, wait, make it two pounds. Yes, two pounds!" It was working, she's doing it, she's getting the meat for her family. Other customers, packages in hand, pass by her for the door. She tries to maneuver the stroller out of the way, and accidentally runs the wheels over an old woman's foot. "Oh, I'm so sorry, I was just trying to get it out of the way."

The white haired lady glares at her.

"I'm sorry, really. Are you OK?"

Again, the silent glare, huddling her small body closer to the counter full of steak and pork. Jesus, she could just say, "That's OK." She could just say, "It's nothing, I'm fine." She could just say something. What does she think, that Sonia purposefully ran the stroller over her fucking foot? God, what is wrong with people? Can't she see that Sonia is trying to shop with two small children, and doesn't she know that it's not an easy thing to do? Can't she see that she doesn't feel well? That she's pregnant? Sonia wants to yell at this old, dried-up bitter bitch. I bet you had kids once, you dumb cow! You just don't remember how hard it was, do you? You just blanked it all out, because it was that awful! Because you sucked at it, too, just like the rest of us! And now, you walk around smug and mean to others who are no different than what you were. And soon you'll be wearing diapers again! Soon you'll be a helpless baby, dependent on some woman in her prime, like my fucking self, to take care of your sorry ass. And then, you'll be dead. Sonia can't take it. It's all too awful. She was just trying to be nice, trying to move her stroller out of the way. What is she supposed to do, leave her kids at home alone while she shops? *Tom and Mike, you stay here by yourselves because children shouldn't be in public places! That's right, stay home alone because I have to buy hamburger. I'll just chain you to the radiator so as not to anger the dumb old ladies in the neighborhood.*

Sonia is fuming. She is having a moment. She can't keep it inside any longer. "You know, you could just acknowledge my apology in some way. It wouldn't kill you to say, that's OK, or something like that. It was an accident as I said, and I apologized to you and the right thing to do is to say something nice back. Not to just glare at me."

This prompts another long, nasty glare, and then the old woman opens her wrinkled mouth, and with a coarse, Brooklyn accent says, "You people think you rule the world. Pushing your strollers all over the place."

"It was an accident! For God's sake, you never pushed a stroller around? You were in a stroller at one point yourself, being pushed around by your mother! Have you no mercy? I'm pregnant, I don't feel well! I'm doing the best I can . . . "

"You come here, you push the real estate market way up, my son has to move to Staten Island because he can't afford it around here anymore, and then you push those strollers down the street like you own the place. This used to be a nice neighborhood."

"Tom, Tom," Sonia says.

Tom is standing quietly, watching his mother with big eyes.

"Ma'am? Your hamburger?"

"Tom, see this lady here? She's got meat inside of her.

And she'll be dead soon. And then she'll just be a piece of meat. Not a person anymore. A piece of old meat, rotting in the ground."

"Ma'am?" The nice Italian man looks at her, with caution in his dark eyes. "Your hamburger is ready."

Mike sleeps on and Sonia pushes the stroller, the bag of hamburger meat hanging from the handle. They are out of milk. She'll get it at the corner deli on the way back to her apartment. This thought makes tears come to her eyes. She has to buy milk and she really doesn't think she can do it. Tom is walking very carefully, deep in thought. Sonia peeks at Mike. A melted Popsicle stick remains clutched in his hand and his hand is curled against his chest. A bright red stain, in the shape of a circle, lies directly where his heart is. Oh, God. Sonia'll never get out that stain. It looks as if he's been shot. A man, an attractive man in a nice suit, carrying a briefcase, walks by and glances down at Mike in the stroller, giving Sonia a scornful look. And now, she can barely push the stroller anymore. She's only three blocks from home, but God, she just can't do it.

"Mommy, why are we walking so slowly?

"Because it's hot, sweetie."

She's standing now. Not walking. She sits down, crossed-legged, the asphalt burning through her black-turning-green cotton pants from the Gap. She is not in the shade. She is in the middle of the sidewalk. It's noon. It's the hottest time of the day, in the hottest city in the world. Sonia is sitting in the hottest, most airless, most inconvenient spot. People walk around her. "Mommy, can we go home?"

"In just a minute. In just a minute."

A young woman, Sonia can't tell how old she is, maybe twenty, maybe thirty, God knows, she could be fifteen, walks by, slowly. She's got big, perky tits, visible through her tight tank shirt. She's wearing jeans, in this heat, tight ones, her flat stomach out for the world to see, her bellybutton small and round and dark. Why is it that Sonia can't tell the difference between a fifteen-year-old and a twenty-five-year-old? Sonia's babysitter, Carrie, is twenty-two, a college student at Brooklyn College, from Trinidad. But she could be thirty for all Sonia knows. She just can't tell anything anymore. All she seems aware of is that her children are very young, she's not, and old people suck shit. The girl, or woman, slows to a stop and says, "Is everything OK?"

But the problem is, she doesn't care. She's got a smug look on her face. Her voice is condescending, not caring. She has a hand on her exposed hip bone. She isn't worried about Sonia. The girl-woman looks at the stain on Mike's shirt. She cares not at all if everything isn't OK. She's lying. Her inquiry is about how she's OK, very OK thank you, and Sonia's not, and that is making her feel good, as she stands there, with her bellybutton winking at Sonia. No, she doesn't care if Sonia is OK at all and this is a big problem.

"I am not really OK. I am pregnant. And I am about to throw up on your shoes."

"You should get some help, lady." She says this, and shifts from one long leg to another.

"Well, that's pretty funny considering that you just asked me if I was OK, and I'm not, clearly, which you already knew. But you didn't ask me if I were OK because you actually wanted to help me, did you? Why ask a question like that? Why mock me when you have no intention of helping me? Is your life that pathetic that you get off on rubbing other people's weaknesses in their face? I am having a bad moment. You're aware of that. And yet, you stand there, so superior. Can't you just be happy with your big tits and be gone? Must you torture helpless, sick pregnant women? "

"Lady, do you want me to call someone?"

"Mommy, can we go cook our meat?"

"No, I don't want you to call anyone. But help me stand up. Just give me your hand. That's all. I can make it. I can make it home. I can." And, awkwardly, not having intended to do so, the young woman stretches out one of her long, tan arms, scented with a sweet, vanilla perfume, and Sonia grabs it like it's a life preserver and she's drowning in the hot, Caribbean Sea, and pulls so hard that the woman nearly topples over. But she doesn't, she braces herself, and Sonia climbs up her arm, all the way to standing, and marches the three blocks home.

———

THAT NIGHT, AFTER SONIA fries hamburger meat for her children and husband, after she herself eats part of a hamburger bun with a little bit of butter on it and drinks flat ginger ale, after the kids fall asleep, and the TV's turned off, Dick and she go to bed. Sonia tries to read *The New Yorker*. This is one of the worst things about being pregnant. She can't read. She can't concentrate. She reads two sentences and then her mind wanders—was that a gas bubble or the baby? when I bumped into the counter tonight, did I hurt the baby? what will I cook for dinner tomorrow? my head hurts so much!—and then she forgets the two sentences she just read. So she tries to read them again. Soon, she's just flipping to the cartoons. Dick puts his hand on her breast.

"It's been months."

"I think weeks. Months? I don't know. You know I don't feel well."

"I'm starving."

"Why don't you fuck your secretary?"

"My secretary? You mean Alex? He's a gay man and I like women."

"I bet he gives a mean blowjob."

"Feel this." He takes her hand away from *The New Yorker* and puts it on his hard dick. He smiles at her, mischievously.

"I hate you right now."

"I like you." He looks at her gently. She's got the upper hand right now. "Could you kiss it?"

"Kiss it?"

"You could start by just kissing it. A little kiss."

"I hate my life. I almost had a nervous breakdown today. A woman at the butcher shop was mean to me. And I couldn't control myself. I sort of freaked out on her. And now I feel like I can never go to the butcher's again."

"Please. Just one little kiss?"

"I'm going to cry, Dick. What if I cried?"

"Just for a few minutes? I won't come in your mouth if you think that'll make you feel sick."

"I hate you. Did you not hear me say that? Are you listening to me at all? I hate you."

"Please? Pretty please?"

I hate you, *I hate you*, thinks Sonia, her head being pushed down the fleshy expanse of her husband's belly. I hate the smell of your cock, the feel of your pubes. I hate your white belly. *I hate you*, she thinks, as she heads south, and begins calculating what he'll owe her for this pleasure.

GIVING ONLY ONE BLOWJOB every three months bestows on Sonia a kind of power over her husband that fucking him regularly doesn't. He deeply appreciates the blow-job. He wakes up with the kids, which he's been doing for months really, but this morning, the morning after the blowjob, he brings her coffee at eight thirty, just how she likes it, with milk and sugar, very warm, maybe he warmed the milk in a pan for her, and when she comes downstairs, the kids are dressed, their teeth brushed, their hair combed, and they've had scrambled eggs for breakfast. The toys are picked up, put away in their little toy bins. The swooshing sound of a load of laundry being washed can be heard from the downstairs bathroom. Dick stands at the sink, scrubbing the pan in which he cooked the eggs. He smiles at her warmly. *Wow*, thinks Sonia. *Wow*. He could do this every morning. He doesn't need me. No one needs me, really. So why doesn't he do this every morning? Because he makes the money and I don't, thinks Sonia? Because he makes the money then it's OK for him to do as little as possible, as much as it takes to get by without completely alienating her. Where, where is the generosity? The apartment glistens at her and it fills her with rage. Why does he only do what it takes? Where is the love?

"Do you want some breakfast, honey?"

"No."

He wants her to say something. He wants her to thank him. Thank you! Thank you for usually doing as little as possible! Thank you for taking advantage of me! For assuming I'll do everything! Thanks for making it clear that when you do something, it's a big fucking favor.

"The kids are dressed."

"I noticed. Why don't you always dress them? Why doesn't the house always look like this before you go to work?"

"What do you mean? I thought you liked getting the kids dressed."

"Fuck you!"

He walks up to her and puts his hand over her mouth, whispering, "Don't talk like that in front of the kids. Just don't."

"I hate my life."

"Man, I can't wait until this part of the pregnancy is over. This is the worst part. You know it, too. You're not rational. You're not well. Your hormones are sending the wrong messages to your brain."

"I hate that you don't do this every morning, don't you see? That this is some kind of favor to me for sucking your dick last night." She's talking quietly now, so the kids can't hear her. But her voice is sharp. "I don't want any favors from you, do you understand that? You either have responsibilities or not. You either give me your best around here, or you don't. And clearly, you usually don't. What makes you the king, huh? Your salary? That's what makes you the king?"

"Hey, if you want to go back to bartending, I'll stay home with the kids. We can live off the great salary you once made. Let's try that out, huh, Sonia? If you want to role-reversal with me, I'll do it. I wouldn't mind the break. Work's not fun you know. It's not a picnic."

"I realize that work is not always fun for you. I realize that. But you are lying when you say you'd quit your job and do what I do. You may have some bad times there, but when it comes down to it, you like what you do. You're good at it. You like going to work, you like coming home and seeing your family, you like someone else doing all that comforting shit when you come home. The dinner. The couch dusted off. The whole shebang."

"I'm sorry, are we supposed to pretend that we could live off of your bartending salary of yore? Is that what you want me to pretend right now?"

"You're not admitting it. You're not admitting what you get out of this deal. I, on the other hand, am taking a look at what I don't get. Why don't I get this? Why is this special? Why don't you give me your best shot every morning? Why don't you feel any obligation around here? All I can say is, I'm never sucking your fucking dick again. You got that? Never."

"I'm calling your shrink. You need to go see your shrink."

Sonia hasn't seen her shrink in years! Not since Tom was born. Dr. Silver, in Brooklyn Heights. It's not a bad idea really, and Sonia thinks she may call him herself. But instead she says, "I'm going to a clinic right now. I'm putting an end to this. I'm not being your wife anymore. Fuck you, you got that? Fuck you and your scrubbing a pan once a month around here shit." Her voice is loud now. Tom and Mike run into the kitchen.

But it's not Sonia who leaves, it's Dick. And she stands mute as he slams the door behind him, the children grabbing onto her legs. Later, when another day is past, when Dick doesn't come home for dinner, but purposefully comes home after the kids are down, Sonia hears him slink into the apartment. The lights are all off and the quiet he gets to come home to enrages Sonia even more. She gives him this, this quiet, but it's not like she has a choice, or does she? She hears him piss downstairs in the bathroom off the boys' room. He doesn't come up to her. She hears him settle on the couch for the night. And then, exhausted, she falls asleep.

7

Carrie comes first thing in the morning and the kids are so happy to see her that Sonia gets depressed. Why do they like their babysitter better than her? Maybe because she takes them to McDonald's? But she doesn't do that every time she comes. Maybe because she entertains them, rather than just takes care of them, which is basically what Sonia does. She doesn't make silly faces or play red light, green light. She just takes care of them.

She's off to see her midwife, the woman who delivered Tom and Mike, for a prenatal checkup. It is so hot and humid outside that the minute Sonia steps outside of her building, she feels like she's been hit with a brick of wetness.

And yet, she is childfree. She moves her legs, her arms sway beside her. Leg, then arm, leg then arm. She's moving. Somewhat effortlessly. She's not pushing anything.

No one is holding her hand. She is . . . free. A smile comes on her face, a twitching smile. Her chin lifts. A noise— a giggle—escapes her mouth. Legs and arms, moving, toward the subway. It's not so hard! It feels good.

And yet, she feels like an imposter. She's not a childfree person. She's pretending to be a childfree person. She is, in fact, paying someone so that she can pretend to be a childfree person. She sits on the F train and it's cool on the train, the air conditioning doing its job. Her nipples get hard under her T-shirt, and she feels like telling the woman reading a book next to her that her kids are with a babysitter. That she isn't what she appears. She's not what she looks like. The woman, of course, doesn't look up from her book, not that Sonia would really say anything to her. A book, now there's an idea. Why doesn't Sonia have a book with her? And then, just as quickly as the thought comes to her, she remembers—because she's pregnant. And when she's pregnant, she can't read. When she's pregnant, she can't think, concentrate, or do anything, really, except sit there and let the fucking thing inside her suck the life out of her. She is deep in thought about how she can't think, so deep, she almost misses switching to the C train. At the last minute, she rushes off the train and catches the other one. Suddenly, her heart hurts. The rushed movement causing a sharp pain. She settles into a spot on the nearly empty train and puts a hand over her heart. It is pumping madly. She can feel it.

The midwives are on the Upper West Side and they are a good lot. Midwives, yes; hippies, no. They believe in epidurals if you want them, they believe in delivering in a hospital, which they do. They are midwives in the European sense, in that they are trained to deliver babies, but they are not surgeons. They are not midwives in the home-birth sense. They are not midwives in the West Coast sense. They don't do C-sections, but a doctor on call could. They are nice. They talk frankly with Sonia, and everyone else, and they've been doing it for twenty-five years now. Jenny is Sonia's midwife. She is a big, round, kind-faced, bespectacled woman from Maine who seems ready to retire. She's been doing this forever. She's good at it, but tired.

"What are you doing back here so soon?" She says to Sonia, as she pulls up a chair.

"I'm pregnant. I'm here for a prenatal checkup."

"You're pregnant again? Didn't I just see you a few months ago for your annual checkup? What happened to that cervical cap? What happened to 'I just want to paint?'" Jenny is looking at her like she's a crazy person and Sonia starts to think she's crazy.

"That cervical cap doesn't work so well."

"I guess not. So why not terminate it?"

"After this Dick's going to get his tubes tied."

"Men don't get their tubes tied."

"You know what I mean. And why is everyone freaked

out about me having another kid? Where's the pro-choice attitude?"

"Hey, you were the one who said no more."

"I'm deeply ambivalent about this baby. Is that what you want to hear? I was deeply ambivalent about the other two, too, you know that."

"Anyone who says they're not is lying. You know that. Love, hate! Love, hate! It's starts in the womb and goes on forever. Anyway, I'll take some blood and check you out and I guess we'll be seeing more of you. How far along are you?"

"Almost done with the first trimester."

"How are the boys?"

"Great." Jenny sticks a needle in her.

"Ow! Jesus, not so rough on me!"

"You with the tattoo on your shoulder. Don't give me that. Three kids! Wow, harking back to the old days."

"Lots of people still have three kids, Jenny."

"I don't know about lots. Are you moving to the sub-urbs?"

"I don't think so. Although I should look around for a bigger apartment."

"Ha! In your neighborhood, not likely. Is this the trying-for-a-girl thing? Is that it?"

"I love my boys. You know that. I'm from a family of girls. I was so happy to have boys."

"Yeah, but now that you have your boys, you want a girl? Is that it?"

"It was an accident and we're just going with it. Dick would love a little girl. I don't know how I feel about it. As long as the little thing is healthy, I'll be happy."

But as Sonia walks down Columbus, looking at the shops full of beautiful clothes she can't wear because soon she'll be as big as a cow, sweating out a particularly pungent sweat due to all the hormones raging in her body in the late summer heat, she thinks, *do I want a girl?* Is this what this is about? To be a mother to a daughter? To, then, relive her own life to a certain extent? To have a little Willa? A passive yet conniving thing? Or worse, to have a little one just like she was, a wild bitchy creature that acted like a boy, but disgraced the family like only a bad girl could?

Another female in the house. Is this what she wants?

No, Sonia likes being the only woman. The alpha female. She loves the warm love of her boys, she loves being surrounded by men, she always has—three men or four men or more. In college, she played cards once a week with a group of guys. Russell, Bob, Jason, Stan. She loved being in that place, a smokey, vulgar place where women rarely were. She loved it. She still does. Her husband and her boys. But what if it's a girl? She hasn't changed the diaper of a little girl since high school. Since she herself was a babysitter. What to do in the face of a little, naked vagina, an innocent pink baby bird of a pussy? God, the thought of it. No, Sonia doesn't want a little girl. She was a little girl herself. Why would she want that?

Her friends, the other mothers in the neighborhood, want girls. Nearly every woman she's met in the playground wants a girl. A girl, just like me! Maybe she'll look just like me! A girl to shop with. A girl for whom to buy pink dresses. One woman—an educated, white, middle-class woman—with three kids, the youngest being a girl, a little thing, maybe eighteen months old, explained, "She helps me pick up after the boys. She's just a baby, but she knows how to pick up. My boys don't, of course." Even now, women still want girls to help them around the house! Sonia doesn't want a girl to help her clean up after her boys. Her boys know how to put away their trains, their dinosaurs, their shoes. What does it mean to think a boy doesn't know how to pick up after himself? What does it mean to think a little girl should pick up after her brothers?

And then her friend Lisa, who explained that she wanted a girl to talk to. Someone she could talk to, because, well, her boys weren't very good communicators. She said this to Sonia, as she clung to her infant daughter. Her sons, listening, playing nearby, looked sadly toward their mother. "You know how men are," said Lisa. "They have no personal skills. They can't listen. They can't talk about their feelings. But Lulu, she'll be my friend! She'll understand what it means to be a woman. We'll have so much in common." Just then, one of her sons threw a car at her. And Sonia thought, *oh, but how men communicate.*

A daughter. The sonogram would tell. A daughter to mock her, to grow young and beautiful while she gets older and less attractive, a daughter who knows just what to say to truly and deeply hurt her. There was a time when women wanted boys. When society worshipped boys. When men wanted sons for the farm. When women wanted boys for their husbands. And now, women want girls. They want more of themselves. They have self-esteem? They love themselves? Or do they just openly get to hate men? No, Sonia would love three boys. Sonia is afraid of women.

Dick, of course, would like a daughter. The dream daughter, someone pretty, someone who, as his wife dries up and ages, he could look to for beauty, for inspiration. Someone who wouldn't identify with him, no, but would just love him. Dick loves his boys very much, but face it, the day would come when they would see their father for who he is—a man, not a God, and a tired, overworked, slightly bored man. And they would be disappointed. But a daughter? She would love him. In his dreams, a daughter would never grow disappointed, disillusioned. Not his daughter, no. And Sonia knows this about Dick. Knows he wants a little girl. Is this why she's going through with this pregnancy? To give her husband what she herself has? The love of the opposite sex? Is she that generous toward him? And what if it's not a girl?

The train is empty. No one reads next to her. She heads back home, her arms loose at her sides. Suddenly, Sonia thinks, I'm alone on this train. Something could happen to me! Where are the other people? The ones to protect me from the bad kind of other people? Do muggers still stalk the subway trains, as they did ten years ago, when she first moved here? But it's the middle of the day. Why is she so frightened? The next stop, and no one gets on. She panics, standing in the cold air. My children! They need me! Swaying as she goes, she heads down the aisle and opens the door to get into the next car, where she hopes there are people. For a moment, she's outside of either car, back in the heat, a dark, horrible heat in a tunnel underground. And then she opens the next door and the light hits her, the cold air-conditioning licks her face. A scattering of three people look up and see a woman, her eyes bugged out in fear, pale and sickly seeming, moving quietly to take a seat on an unoccupied bench.

Tom and Mike. She needs them. They make her less afraid. She feels naked and vulnerable without them. Clinging to her purse, she thinks, *But once, a long time ago, I was alone in the world. And I wasn't afraid.*

The sonogram appointment is set. The blood work is done. It all feels so official. A baby, a baby. One more and then no more.

8

The first trimester ends one morning. Just like that, Sonia wakes up and the light through the skylight above is less harsh and the room feels fresh. The air in her loft is not moist, is not stuffy. Summer is over. Her sickness is over. It is fall. It is the real new beginning, the real beginning of this pregnancy. It is September, God bless. She stands and stretches, and where is Dick? Already making her coffee, already with the boys. She goes to the bathroom and pulls down her underwear and sits and pees and she just can't believe it—she is not sick anymore. She is better. It's over, just like that. Just like the first time and just like the second time, one day she is sick, as she's been for three solid months, and then the next day she is not. She is no longer nauseated, she is no longer miserable, her head no longer hurts. Her mouth is warm and pasty, like a morning mouth, but not dry and disgusting, with the stink of wet garbage. It's over! The first trimester is over! She skips downstairs and her husband stands at the counter, glancing fearfully toward her and she smiles at him, and then she grabs her coffee and kisses her boys, one at a time, first little Mike, then Tom, and then she takes her coffee and heads for the living room and and—it's over! She's not sick. Lord above, heavens above, she is better. She looks out the window and then bends to open it—this she can do, she can bend to her low window and pull it upward, it's stiff and old, but she can do it, she's not sick!—and the air comes in and it's sweet like fresh hay, this Brooklyn September air. It's the cleanest, freshest air she's ever smelled, ever felt against her skin. And goosebumps rise on her arms, and they are bumps of joy, bumps from the crisp air that she herself managed to bring into this room, not from the cold, clammy sickness that just yesterday, made her feel as if she'd rather die than anything else. That she would never make it. That she was not going to make it through another day. No, no these prickly, risen pores on her skin line her arms and the back of her neck because life is a good thing now, a very good thing, and everything is going to be alright and the air is fresh and the birds in the still green trees sing to her and her alone! And Sonia wants to cry for joy but she has no tears. Dick walks up to her now, from behind, and he doesn't quite touch her because she hasn't wanted him to touch her for months now, and he says, "How's the coffee?"

"It's great. And I feel great. I feel better now. You know how it is. Just like that." Sonia says to her husband, the dear man of her house, and she turns to him and gently puts her hand on his arm.

AND THAT NIGHT, AFTER the kids pass out in their bunk-beds downstairs, goodnight Tom, goodnight Mike, sleep well, who loves you?, who loves you the most?, one more kiss, one more kiss; then after Sonia and Dick finish watching a sitcom on TV, after Sonia drinks a warm chamomile tea, after Dick sips his scotch on ice, after they brush their teeth, relieve their bladders, and slide into the clean white, cotton sateen sheets Sonia put on that very day, Dick leans into Sonia's face and kisses her. First he kisses her on her cheek, on the part of the cheek that is right next to her mouth. Then he moves in closer to her lips, touching the corner of her mouth with his mouth. She turns toward him now, in the dark, her eyes closed, and he leans his upper body over hers and turns his face so his nose won't get in the way and he pushes his mouth against hers and, open-mouthed, they kiss. Their tongues reach out and taste, and damn, if it doesn't taste good. Damn if it doesn't taste like warmth, like booze and like that familiar flavor that is each other. This is not a night when Dick will fart obscenely in bed next to her, pretending not to, and Sonia, despising him, will snap her magazine angrily into a perfect tent in front of her face. Nor is it a night, like so many before this one, where Sonia, stinking of sweat from the summer heat, from the sweat of fear and the sharp stink of bile and vomit, is so disgusting, no, not disgusting, so *terrifying*, terrifying in her foreignness, in her stink, in her pale, ugly, possum-in-a-trap look on her face, that Dick just wouldn't look at her.

Those first three months are over. Those three months of hell, where Dick would just pretend she was not there, gone. Done. She'd be there, and he'd pretend, just like he did as a child when his father was yelling, or his mother was yelling, that the person in question was not there. Dick's imagination is so powerful and has always been so powerful, that he can play this trick in his brain very well and Sonia knows this about him, even if he doesn't know it about himself.

No, not tonight. Tonight he had looked at her on the couch, lazing with him in front of the TV, and she could feel his appreciation, his desire. She feels she is the woman he fell in love with. She feels his eyes on her and she's the same young woman she was fifteen years ago, she's no different than she was when she was barely twenty. The bones in her face are strong but womanly, her mouth feels wet and inviting, her eyes are smart but slightly troubled, definitely knowing. Often thinking of something dirty. She's still his dirty-minded college girl. And this, in the dark now, now that she is over that first part of her preg-nancy, now that she no longer repulses him, hates him,

now that she is resigned to her body and the strange creature inside of it, this bud of a person that he planted in
her womb, now that this baby isn't torturing her anymore,
now she wants to get fucked. Her skin is powdered with
stardust, it's fucking moist, damn it, and sparkling, and her
eyes are wet like a healthy cat's, glowing at her husband
in the dark, open now, looking at him while their tongues
stroke the insides of their mouths like they've never tasted
each other before.

How could kissing this man be anything that ever happened again? After years of marriage, years of just fucking, not that anything's wrong with that, but years really
where they would never, ever have kissed. Preferring to
get straight to the part that matters, kissing having bored
them, kissing having been something of the past. Kissing
not being on their minds but they still needed to get off.
His balls would fill. She was the nice lady next to him who
empties them for him. She often felt his gratitude, but she
had stopped feeling his wonder. Excitement. Urgency.
Except during these precious months when she was pregnant with their first son. And their second son. And then
again, later, when the nursing starts and her breasts fill
with milk. These special interludes, when Sonia is not
quite Sonia, but something very close. And now, again, this
gift. This time, this fleeting moment in their banal lives.

Here he is, his hands on her breasts which are so swollen, so sensitive she moans and pulls away slightly and she

loves her own tits right now so much, she can't believe they are hers. A few months ago they were dried out, with tired nipples that lay nearly flat against her ribcage. Her breasts, when she's not pregnant, were never as fleshy as her upper arms. It would be jangly arms and flat breasts. Now she can only see breasts. She has breasts! Serious breasts. He has one in his hand and another in his mouth and she's shaking now, because all those hormones that are making her breasts grow into these beautiful flowers are making them raw with nerves. He's being gentle with her, she feels. Well, he's trying to be gentle, precisely because she's making it clear, Sonia is, how painful her swollen breasts are. He squeezes and sucks them and she can't stay still, she's just squirming, it's uncomfortable but undeniable, she breathes out the word ouch, and she puts her own hand on them to protect herself, but also to feel them herself. Because these breasts are a gift from God, the God who gave humans the ability to reproduce, and to feed their young. These tits are blessed and she wants to hold them too.

He arches his entire body over her now, he's up on his knees, not leaning his body on hers, no, looking right at her, and he locks his mouth on hers again and fuck, she's kissing her goddamn husband. She wants to lick out the inside of his fucking throat. And then he puts his finger in her pussy, just like that, and she's wet and warm. She nearly comes right then. But he pulls away from her and takes a deep breath. On his knees now he grabs his dick hard and pushes at it. Oh, man. Her skinny legs are splayed out from the bowl of her small hips, and in the dark she stares at his enormous erection. Jesus. She can't look at it. She looks away. If he puts his dick in there now, she'll just come right away and that is not what she wants to do. But what else can they do now? He could eat her pussy, but she doesn't really want that, strangely, and she's pretty certain he won't, for some reason. It's about his dick tonight, about the effect she's having on his dick. He turns her over and she can feel him assessing her ass, which he loves, always professing his love for her ass. But it's calming him a bit, Sonia can feel his body relax, her ass is familiar, not strange and new like her breasts right now and it's not her fucking wet pussy staring at him either. But she can't help herself, she lifts it up at him and there's no hiding from what's underneath it. He leans over her and he rubs his dick on her like a cat in heat and then she's rubbing her ass back at him, Sonia feels like begging him, she is begging him with her ass, begging him to stick it in her, which he does—sticks it into her—and he leans over her and takes each one of those breasts in his hands. And then he grabs both breasts in one hand, smashing them together hard, and she lets out a short cry, and with his free hand he grabs her head and twists it around toward him so that he can shove his tongue down her mouth again. Damn. Damn.

Oh, if she were only always pregnant! Oh, if she were

always four months, five months, even six months pregnant! Not one or two or three! And not seven or eight or nine! But that middle time, this middle time, how she loves it, how she can't believe it's her, how ripe she is, how womanly, how soft and precious and giving and forgiving she is! Oh, if she could only stay this fleshy, this wet, this ready. If only she were always in a dark room, if only her breasts were always like this in a dark room. Then, then her life would be perfect. Locked away in a dark room, a room which only her husband had the key to, permanently four months pregnant.

This whole putting things off is not working. She turns herself over again, and her breasts flop around in a good way, move like jello, loose and real, and there are her hip bones, her splayed legs, and he gently thumbs her clit but she pushes his hand off of her pussy and arches up to him, her own hands on her tits, moaning and he grips her hips and thrusts in there deep and she knows he's about to come. It's just gonna happen. Her head is twisted to the side and her own hands smash her breasts together—they touch! They're so big they touch each other! He thrusts again and she can feel he's so close and he can come inside her if he wants, she's already pregnant, it's not going to make her more pregnant, and she loves everything about this, the no condom, the no cervical cap, the no smelly spermicidal jelly, just the thick, salt smell of his dick in her pussy and he can come inside of her if he wants, she thinks.

But then he lifts his dick out and holds it over her breasts, his knees up near her armpits now and one hand on his pulsing cock, and the other grasping her round, fleshy breasts together, and he shoots come all over her round, round breasts, banging his cock against her, then—*tap, tap, tap*—knocking out every last drop of himself onto her. And Sonia is, in no small way, the happiest woman on earth, the womanliest woman on earth, wet with come, pregnant and fucked like only a woman can be, so simple and animal and perfect, God's perfect creation.

THE NEXT MORNING, NOT so early, the days getting noticeably shorter, autumn light, pale but clean, shines through the skylight above their spent bodies, a thin cashmere blanket cocooning them from the slight chill in the room. Sonia wakes first and looks at her husband sleeping huddled at the other end of the bed. When she wakes, she's very awake, suddenly, as sometimes happens. No slow opening to the world, no desire to stay in bed and shut her eyes and try for more. No, she's up. Stealthily, she heads downstairs to make the coffee. Standing in the doorway adjoining the kitchen to the boys' bedroom is Mike, her little one, a soggy diaper hanging from his bottom and a too small T-shirt showing his round belly and outie bellybutton. He's standing there, having just woken himself and having started off to fetch a grown-up and having not woken his older brother. Sonia scoops him up and Mike leans his soft head on her shoulder and she breathes her warm morning breath into her son's perfect, sweet neck. The kitchen is dark but comforting. Walking this way, with her young boy in her arms, she sets about to making coffee, balancing Mike on her hip and doing everything else with one hand, so as not have to put down her son. So she can keep this warm, wet-bottomed bundle in her arms as she does what needs to be done. And life is good. Life is very good. And Sonia is thankful for her family, eager for her precious, mediocre life, and she can't believe that once again, she's going to be a mother to someone new.

9

Mike, her little one, her baby, starts preschool at the same little preschool where Tom goes. Three mornings a week, Sonia packs up the kids, pushes the stroller down the street two blocks, and drops them both off. No having to call Carrie. Nobody comes into her house, which is great, since it tends to be a huge mess. There they go, running with excitement, into a room full of blocks and plastic toys and art projects and other little people, the same size as them. The first day Sonia dropped them both off, it was as if she'd done that weird trick where you press your arms hard against the inside of someone else's arms, and you both clench your fists and push and push until the other person pulls their arms away and your arms float upward. Without having to do anything, without actually trying to move your arms toward the sky, they just go. Flying high. A freaky, uncontrolled feeling. But fun. She had been afraid, ashamed, worried. What if Mike hates it there? And then she thought, yeah, he really wants to be home with me all day, watching too much TV and staring at the same four walls for sixteen hours. He really wants to go grocery shopping with me instead of sing the itsy bitsy spider with ten other drooling two-year-olds. And then she thought, *what if some other little brat hits him?* And then the counter thought: *Tom's never, ever hit Mike. So, gee, that would be a new experience. Ha.*

After two more days of dropping him off, she decided to completely relax about it instead of trying to think of reasons to not be relaxed about it. It goes smoothly this time. She spent a solid month freaking out about Tom when Tom started preschool. Tom developed a case of hives due to witnessing his mother break into a sweat every time she dropped him off. Mike, lucky Mike, misses out on a lot of her neurotic energy. Three days of bewilderment, and then, freedom. Freedom for Mike that is. And for Sonia, too, a sort of freedom. But Sonia doesn't feel totally free. Free from freaking out about preschool, yes. But, there's her amniocentesis appointment today. There's the fact that the last sonogram showed that everything looks fine, but her baby was "shy" and they couldn't tell if it was a girl or a boy and so when she gets the amnio, she'll know for sure. She never had to get an amnio with her other kids because she wasn't yet thirty-five, and there were no indications otherwise via blood work. Now, she's thirty-five.

All thirty-five year olds get amnios. And so, after she meets
Clara and some other mothers for a coffee, she's going to
her appointment.

September! The air is suddenly clean. Sonia is hungry, happy, feels like she may be the luckiest person in the
world. She loves her tits, she loves the fall. Her skin has
that glow and she knows it. She wears a long sleeve shirt
for a change and her same pants, which are starting to get
a little tight, and she's a bit chilly. Soon, it'll be time for a
jacket. And some maternity clothes, really. The construction men have packed their bags and repaved the sidewalks. There is less dust. Less noise. No overbearing heat.
She walks, hands free, a little blue bag over her shoulder,
to the breakfast place on Court Street where she's meeting Clara and Risa. She looks in the windowpanes of the
stores as she goes, watching her figure, and she thinks, *I'm
not big yet, but I feel good.* The women are sitting by the
window—she's the last to get there. Sonia's told Clara that
she can tell people she's pregnant. She's past the miscar-
rying stage, for the most part. Now, the amnio will tell
Sonia whether or not the fetus has Down's syndrome, as
well as a whole host of other genetic abnormalities, and
if the fetus has Down's syndrome, she has the opportu-
nity to abort. But, Sonia, oddly, is not afraid that the baby
has Down's syndrome. Or not afraid enough to not let it
be known to the world that she is pregnant. In her mind,
Sonia imagines that things could be wrong with the baby,

but nothing so obvious as Down's syndrome. The baby may be a crazy bitch, may have Tourette's syndrome, may be a psycho serial killer, but Down's syndrome is not one of Sonia's fears. Soon she'll know as much as they can tell her, which Sonia thinks is not a lot. And, in the meantime, she's ready to have it be official, to have it be public. She's pregnant. Let the world know, she's pregnant.

"Congratulations!" says Risa, as Sonia sits down. Clara smiles, beaming proudly, almost as if she were the father.

"Do you know if it's a girl?" asks Risa.

"No, they couldn't tell during the first sonogram. But I have my amnio today, so I will find out soon."

"Pray for a girl!" Risa, leaning into the table now, with a fierceness in her voice. "I didn't feel like a real mother until I had my daughter. You know what they say, a son's a son until he takes a wife, a daughter's a daughter, for all your life."

"Well, my boys are far from getting married so I feel like a mother or whatever. I'm kind of scared of having a daughter. I love my boys. Either way. I mean, I don't care that much. Or, I don't know. I would be very proud to have three boys. As long as the baby is healthy, isn't that how it goes?"

"My husband and I bought the book on how to have sex so that it's a girl. I could've given it to you! It worked for us. You have sex at the very end or very beginning of the cycle, and you stay on top, and when he comes, you have him pull his penis almost out of your vagina. Oh, and you can't have an orgasm," Risa explains.

"Wow. That sounds like a lot of fun," Sonia deadpans.

"You see, the semen need to swim further so all the Y chromosomes die, or something like that. And, I must say, having a daughter changes your life," says Risa. A sleeping infant swaddled in pink lays next to her in a stroller. "Everything about my daughter is amazing. She's only six months old but already I can tell she's intelligent and kind. It's just so different, having a little girl."

"This was an accident. So your book wouldn't have been that helpful."

"Come on, you want a girl, admit it," says Clara.

"If I had a choice, which I don't, I probably would choose a girl. For my husband, really. And I guess, because it's different than what I already have. But remember, I'm from a family of girls, two daughters, an overbearing mother. Our fucking dog was a girl. Having boys has been really fun for me. I've always and forever loved boys. I still do."

"Everyone needs a daughter," says Clara. "Who's going to take care of you when you get old? Your sons? I don't think so."

"Clara, I don't want a daughter so that I'll have a free nursemaid of sorts for my old age." Sonia manages to make eye contact with the waitress. She orders an omelet, bacon, coffee, and a large juice. Her appetite is back. She's ravenous, always.

"Wow, you must be feeling better," says Clara.

"I am. Finally. I feel great. I love life again!"

"Those first few months are a bitch," says Risa.

"I'm not vomiting all the time, I like food. Mike started preschool. I probably should be looking for a new apartment. But in general, life is good. Dick is being wonderful. I don't hate my husband right now. Fuck, I'm so content I'm almost bored."

"You won't be bored soon. A new baby will end that." Clara says.

"No doubt. Babies keep you busy," Risa says. "What preschool does Mike attend?"

Sonia senses something she doesn't like. Sonia hates the school talk. It makes her want to move back to the Midwest.

"Tom and Mike go to Open Arms Nursery. That little place down Atlantic."

A look nearing alarm crosses Risa's face. "Oh," she says, her eyes darting across the room.

"My theory is, it's preschool. It doesn't matter so much. As long as they're having fun."

"Fun?" Clara says. "Preschool is a very important time. It's not about fun. It's about developing the skills that will carry your child through the rest of his or her life."

"Well, that's not really how I look at it."

"Sam was just diagnosed with ADHD and we're getting together a whole proper medical approach to it. Brooklyn Fellowship is really on top of things that way. Nothing gets by them. I would never send my kid to some place that doesn't have the proper developmental approach to early childhood needs. If you don't catch things early, there's no hope for your children. I'm just thankful they caught Sam's problem early enough," Clara says.

"Attention Deficit Disorder? What is he supposed to be paying attention to? He's four years old."

"Some four-year-olds can read, you know," adds Risa sternly.

"Well who gives shit about some four-year-olds. Some four-year-olds still crap in their pants. Some four-year-olds are ten feet tall. Whatever."

Sonia's food arrives. She starts shoveling it down.

"All I know is I want the best for my child. Why be a parent unless you make sure they get the best of everything available?" Risa says.

"I agree with you, Risa," says Clara. "Sam's doctors are giving him the most advanced treatment available in the world. I wouldn't have it any other way."

Sonia's bacon has already disappeared. "What's that mean, the most advanced treatment?" she asks, her voice muffled by eggs.

"New forms of Ritalin. They just keep making it better, improving on the original medication."

"Oh Clara, no! Really? I spend time with Sam"—and here Sonia pauses, because she does think he's sort of a wreck—"he's not that bad. He's doing fine."

Clara daintily picks at her salad. "He's not doing fine, Sonia. But I know you mean well."

"But drugs? Can we use the word drugs? I prefer the word drugs. Medication is so—dry. Don't put him on drugs right away. What about behavioral therapy?"

"Come on, Sonia, you've seen Sam. He can't pay attention to anything. The medication was the school's idea, but I'm behind them a hundred percent. All the other kids at his school have started reading and he jumps from one activity to another. He can't focus! You just got lucky with Tom. And you should watch what you say, too, because what if something happens to Mike? What if he doesn't develop properly? What if he starts behaving oddly? What if his preschool teachers say to you, we need to talk? You'd fall on your knees. You'd do everything and see every specialist available. You would."

"But you were just saying a couple of months ago that Sam watches too much TV and his dad is never around and you are totally overwhelmed. Couldn't any of that have to do with his attention problems? At least try making some changes at home first, before putting him on the drugs," says Sonia.

Clara laughs. "Blame the mother! I'm a bit shocked that this is coming from you, Sonia. You, the fierce feminist freethinker type. Autism used to be blamed on the mother being cold and unemotional. Can you imagine?"

Sonia is so pissed she wants to spit the eggs her mouth is filled with at her friend. "Feminism doesn't eschew responsibility! Not in my mind. You stick your son in front of the TV for five hours a day, so take responsibility for that. That's got to do something to his brain."

Clara is unmoved. "Whatever you think of TV-watching, that preschool you send your children to sucks. I would never, ever send my kid there. Something could be terribly wrong with Tom or Mike and they wouldn't even know. Child development is not on their agenda."

Risa says, "Getting my son Henry properly diagnosed has been the best thing that happened to us."

"What exactly is wrong with your son?" Sonia asks, but she doesn't really want to know. Not for the first time, she hates the fact that she is raising her kids in New York, where people treat their children like a combination between a science and an art project.

"He has Unclear Developmental Disorder. A disorder mostly found in young boys. It's becoming more and more common. He used to keep to himself a lot, and only play with certain types of toys."

"What types?" Sonia asks.

"Cars."

"Cars?"

"Henry was really missing out," Clara says.

"Yes," Risa says, "He was missing out on normal child-hood. You should have seen him. It wasn't like he played with cars and then went on to play with other kids. He, like, just played with cars."

Clara says, slapping the table, "You've got to take your kids out of that preschool, Sonia. God knows what could be wrong with them. You'd never know. And early intervention is the most important thing."

"You have no idea what it's like to have a child with special needs," Risa says. "It's daunting. But thank goodness for all the resources available to us now. Henry gets his occupational therapy, speech therapy, play therapy. They have a whole host of specialists who can really cater to his needs."

"He's three! Three-year-olds aren't supposed to have a wide range of interests!"

Risa says, very seriously now, "He's four. You really, really need to take your boys out of that place. God knows what could be afflicting them."

Suddenly, Sonia understood that she hated these women. How quickly they slumped themselves into sexless, materialistic gossips. How all of their ambitions became ruthlessly projected onto their defenseless children and husbands. How anything that threatened their idea of family—imperfect children, poor black people, Hispanic immigrants, tacky clothing, lack of social prowess—alarmed them into muteness. How bragging that their husbands never changed a diaper made them feel powerful. How truly so very little changed, unless, and only unless, you dreamed to live outside of their world. And then where did that leave you? Nowhere. Alone. Exactly where Sonia belonged. Perhaps what she hated most was their complete lack of doubt. Clara and Risa utterly believed in what they were; that the best private schools were what their children deserved, though children all around them went to crowded public schools and had no other choice.

Clara and Risa believed in their inheritances. They believed in staying at home and shopping. They believed that they were their husbands' wives and their children's mothers. And those who didn't believe didn't have the same God. Those who didn't believe weren't saved.

Sonia's plate is clean. She thanks Clara and Risa, and tells them it's time for the amnio.

"Good luck, Sonia" says Clara. "Call me if you need me! And call me anyway, because I want to know if it's girl!"

Sonia tells Clara she'll call her later.

As she walks out the door, Sonia thinks she just wants to move to the Midwest. To get away from this neurotic New York shit. But what does she know about the Midwest? She hasn't been there in years. It could be just as bad as this place. Maybe the whole world has gone mad.

A FEW BLOCKS AWAY, a woman in a white coat sticks an abnormally large needle into her belly and pulls out a large vat of fluid. Sonia feels like a turkey. Her midwives don't do amnios, so she's at a clinic near her apartment. A doctor, or a technician, or someone official comes in with a chart. "You'll hear from us soon with the results. How are things going in general?"

"Fine. I'm not throwing up anymore so I'm quite happy. Did you see if it's a boy or a girl by any chance?"

"It's a girl."

"Are you sure?"

"Yeah, it was a vagina. On a fetus, the genitals are quite swollen so there's no mistaking it. It's definitely a girl." He flips some papers around on his chart. "Is that a good thing?"

"Uh, yeah. I guess so. Wow. A girl. I have two boys."

"Well now you'll get your girl."

"Yeah, I guess so." For some reason, Sonia is stunned.

The doctor says, "Go home and drink some wine and relax. Just a glass or two, but it can help prevent miscarriage."

"All right, I'll do that." Sonia rubs the gooey gel on her stomach with a dry, nervous hand and then pulls her shirt over her belly, which suddenly seems larger than ever. She'll need to buy maternity clothes. God help her, it's a girl. It's a girl. After picking up her boys from school, she heads home, drinks some wine. She lets them watch television. She waits. And when Dick arrives, she walks up to him where he stands in the door and hugs him and whispers into his neck, "It's a girl, Dick, they say it's a girl."

10

The light in the apartment changes dramatically. The occasional heat and bright sun of the summer that lingers into September is gone for good. It's darker now. The heat and light of the day have a faded quality, and orange and yellow leaves in the backyard contain more brightness than the sky itself. Sonia's stomach is round, low in the cavern of her abdomen, as she always carries. She looks pregnant, but barely—she's carrying very small this time. She's officially with child. The baby moves and now there is no mistaking this for anything else, not for gas bubbles or cramps, although those things are starting in, too, as her digestive equipment is smushed upward into her lungs and throat. Her daughter is taking up room, leaving less space for her own insides.

The boys are happy in preschool and the ease which Sonia knew was coming her way, with her two kids gone three mornings a week, feels painful to her. *This isn't really happening*, she thinks. This is just for a few months. (And then there is this strange emptiness. They don't need me anymore. And then Sonia rubs the small mound of her stomach. A new excuse on the way.) A strange feeling of freedom, followed by fear of it—what would I ever do with myself?—followed by, it's all ending soon. Very soon. Why bother trying to set up an easel? Why bother sketching, when there's a new crib to be found, because they gave the old one away, because they weren't going to have any more babies? When there are prenatal checkups to schedule? And where are they going to put that crib anyway? Where are they going to live?

The first week of October Sonia goes apartment hunting. This proves horribly depressing, as it always was. She looks out in Kensington, a solid forty minutes on the F train away from Cobble Hill. There, they could afford a three or even four bedroom house. With a parking space. The community is ethnically diverse, consisting of Russian and Mexican immigrants, the schools are good, but both she and Dick would miss the sophistication of Cobble Hill. The Manhattany vibe in Cobble Hill. Most people in Kensington live and work in Brooklyn. Most people in Cobble Hill work in Manhattan. This is a big difference. Really, it's a matter of socioeconomic class: Sonia doesn't want to be part of a serious minority. She doesn't want Tom and Mike to be nearly the only kids from an English speaking, middle-class family. She's ashamed of these feelings, but has them nonetheless. And then there's Dick's commute. He would have to leave so early in the morning that he'd barely see his kids for all of ten minutes. And he'd get back so late that he'd barely be able to kiss them goodnight before they passed out. And Sonia relies greatly on those few hours a day Dick now has with his sons.

Despite Sonia's fear of the commute, she decides to look out in the super-leafy, more leafy than Brooklyn, suburbs of New Jersey. She gets Carrie to pick up the boys from school while she drives around with a middle-aged, forty-pounds-overweight broker in Maplewood. Here, the schools are dubbed as "excellent, truly excellent" but Sonia gets the idea that that really means all white, all middle class. And as much as she feared being a minority in Kensington, she fears even more being literally stranded among people who are supposedly just like her. She's never felt that anyone was just like her, regardless of skin color or money—it's just not a dream she could ever buy into. It doesn't ring any bell for her. Everyone looks sour and scared to Sonia, as she leans slightly out of her window, letting the autumn breeze blow her hair straight up in weird tufts. The houses are expensive. They are lifelong projects. When would she ever paint? Never. She would be too busy worrying about gutters, the lawn and shopping to furnish the many rooms.

After five houses, the broker drives her back to the train

station. With the red, pointy nails of a chubby hand, she indicates the church she attends, but—perhaps realizing her passenger is not a churchgoer—adds, "Oprah says your house is where your soul needs to find comfort."

It is at this moment that Sonia has a panic attack. It starts with her heart pounding with fear. She is hyperventilating too, but not aware of it. She just thinks, *get me away from here. I need to get away from here.* Her face flushes a dark crimson. Her mind swirls. The broker looks like she's in a plastic bubble and her voice sounds as if it's coming from miles away.

"Are you OK?" she asks.

Sonia nods, she can't speak. She's suffered from panic attacks on and off in her life. She knows it will soon be over. This trip to New Jersey, this car ride with the broker.

"You looked awfully flushed," says the Oprah-loving, churchgoing broker.

"I need to get back on the train. A train back to the City."

"Do you want to see one more house?"

"No. I need to get back on a train, please." Her voice comes out so calmly, but inside, she's screaming.

Sonia nods again and starts doing the deep breathing exercises she learned long ago, when she saw Dr. Silver for the attacks. She also used to carry around a paper bag, to breathe into, so as to help her overoxygenated brain return to normal.

What if she has to start carrying a paper bag around all the time again? That was such a sad time in her life, having to go into bathrooms at parties or at work and inhale deeply into a paper bag. It worked, but it made her feel like a loser.

ON THE TRAIN RIDE back to the city, the baby inside her moves around, doing somersaults, no doubt. Sonia feels like her body is someone's indoor swimming pool, not her own body anymore. How is Sonia going to find comfort in a house? Her body is somebody's house and there is nothing comforting about that. The whole thing fills her with rage. The thought of a house! A big, needy thing that everyone knows you live in. The social presence of it! If Sonia bought a house, even in Kensington, she decides that it would eat her alive. No house! No comfort for her soul! No suburbs. No nothing. Just her nice two-bedroom apartment. Just some sameness during this time of more change. Another person arriving forever! And a daughter at that. The change of it fills Sonia with dread. It makes her miss her boys already. It will be even worse than when Mike was born. The anger she felt toward little needy Tom, as she tried to breastfeed. And Tom's little disappointed face, as once again, his mother pushed him aside. "Not now! Tom. Can't you see I'm busy with the baby?" And the minute the words came out of her mouth, the deep regret and shame. The complete lack of control.

As Sonia remembers it, she barely made it through that time. Barely. She'd been so tired, she had no energy for her little, needy toddler. Babies had a way of sucking out her energy. The constant holding, the constant waking up at night. Waah! Waah! Oh, if only she had a wet nurse! But even then, even with tons of help, the real problems were emotional, like always. Because it was not like your heart immediately opened up and grew larger for the new child. No, it was a much more grueling process than that. It was a new, strong annoyance at the older child. It was stabbing, hateful guilt at those feelings. It was a falling in love with the new baby and becoming ever so slightly disappointed in the older child. With a baby, you see the faults of the older child more vividly. The baby is perfect! The child already has imperfections—the child is human. The baby is beyond human. It had been so hard! But she'd survived it, somehow made it so she loved and cared for two. But three? And a girl? Now she'll have to be the role model, not just the mother. Now she'll have to set an *example*. This horrifies her, to no end. Keeps her up at night. Keeps her dreaming of escape. She doesn't want to try to make more room in her heart for another child. She feels full enough. She has two hands for her two boys. She has a lap big enough to hold both of them at the same time. And now, and now where would the stray one go? And who would that stray one be? Would it be Mike, the middle one, lost in the shuffle? Or Tom, the oldest, always being forced to be independent and behave well?

Dread starts to give Sonia weird rashes on her neck at night that go away by the morning. The fear of her future plants itself in her, spreading deep roots. She is in the grip of a huge change, the ushering of a new life into the world, and she's not up to it. No, not at all.

SONIA BUYS A SMALL crib from Ikea and puts it next to their bed up in the loft. She'll deal with moving later. Later, maybe, she'll look for an apartment in Red Hook. Or in Tucson. Or in Madison, Wisconsin. Portland, Oregon. Now, when she has a moment during preschool hours, when she's not at the midwife's, when she's not busy with some other chore, she goes to the bookstore and buys books on various places to live. Bayfield, Wisconsin! On the edge of Lake Superior, near Canada, surrounded by national parks. Gay men and artists abound! Or Birmingham, Alabama. A small rock music scene there, the band Verbena, for instance. Weird, southern hippies and beautiful old houses. South Bend? No, not South Bend. But, northern Michigan, on Lake Charlevoix! Where Hemingway once summered. Dick would listen politely to her tales of all these various places.

"What about Cuba? We could learn Spanish. The schools are great."

"There is no food there. It's poor. What a horrible idea."

"The architecture is great. Prostitution is rampant. I would feel at home there. Secretaries are prostitutes."

"You could make more money selling yourself here."

And then, another night, Sonia says, "What about Jamaica? We could become potheads. And grow leathery skin from the sun."

Dick sighs at his wife and puts his hand on one of her breasts. He strokes her, downward, his dry hand caressing her round stomach. "Let's fuck," he says his fingers heading south.

Sonia says, "I'm nearing the end of this time. The end of the having sex all the time time." Dick's fingers lay delicately inside her. He thumbs her clit.

"Ow! That was too rough. I'm just getting to be at the supersensitive stage. Or something."

"I'll be gentle," he whispers in her face.

Sonia puts her hands over her face and the smell of her skin disturbs her. She smells yeasty, like sourdough bread. She sniffs her palms, the sides of her fingers. Did she touch something weird before she got in bed? No, she remembers washing her hands right before bed. This fermented smell is coming from her skin. She pulls her hands away and looks at them in the dark. They seem thick with veins and fluid. They will only get more so. They seem pulsing and generating some energy, and Sonia sits up, panicky, looking at the growing mound of her body.

"I smell weird."

"No, you don't, honey. Lie back. What's wrong?"

"I don't know if my body can do this again. Give birth. God, I feel like something is wrong."

"You're pregnant. You're doing a great job. I know it's hard."

"You don't know how hard it is. And I'm not doing a 'great job.' I haven't done anything, except fuck you. This is happening to me, don't you understand? I have nothing to do with it. It's taking over me. It's taking over my body and my soul, for God's sake, like some parasite, like some alien virus." Tears come to her eyes.

Dick becomes preternaturally calm. "I know I don't know what it's like to be pregnant. I'm sorry, I didn't mean to belittle your experience. What I meant is that you're being brave in the face of it, and I know, from your two other pregnancies, that it's a hard time for you."

"I don't want to have sex." Her voice is little, defeated.

"OK. Of course. If you don't want to."

ON THE WEEKENDS, DICK takes the car out of the garage and drives the family upstate. They stay in family resorts and watch the leaves turn every variation of orange. They drive to the Poconos without making any reservations and find a rambling place with a pond called O'Brien's.

Sonia says, as the children run around, throwing sticks into the muddy water, "People live out here. They work and they live out here."

"You would die of boredom here," Dick says. "You'd have nothing in common with the other mothers out here."

"I'm not so sure I have anything in common with the mothers in Brooklyn. Or with anybody anywhere."

"Sonia, don't say things like that."

"Why not? Because you don't want to know that I'm feeling alienated and afraid?"

"I do want to know how you are feeling, but making blanket statements like 'I have nothing in common with anybody' isn't very helpful. Nor is it realistic. What can I do with that kind of information?"

"Listen. Just listen to me. I don't need any answers or advice."

"You don't want to move to the Poconos. Neither do I, for that matter."

"I'm mostly resigned to staying in our apartment for now. I think it's the best thing for now. But eventually, and maybe sooner rather than later, we'll need to make some change. And I think a big change would be a good one."

"Well let's deal with that when the time comes. Can't we just be in the Poconos and enjoy visiting the country? Can't we not pretend that we're moving everywhere we visit? I mean, are these weekend trips a bad idea or something?"

"No, I enjoy these trips. They just get me thinking about the possibilities in life. And that's good. And sometimes, in Brooklyn, I feel like I have no possibilities."

"Well, that's all in your mind. Possibilities are everywhere. Don't blame the place you live. If you need to make a change, you will. And things are changing all on their own, too. This baby will change our lives, undoubtedly." Dick sighs, inscrutably. The boys are running around, stopping to look at things as mundane as clumps of dirt and sticks. It's all foreign and exciting to them. The narrowness of city life is so evident to Sonia right now. And yet, she knows it goes both ways. She knows because she's from Indiana.

"You know, Dick, not so long ago you said to me that you can't quit your job now and make some big life change because we have another child coming. So understand that I feel stuck, too. That having another kid is making us both feel stuck."

"OK. I'll grant you that. But I don't want to leave New York. Or Brooklyn. And neither do you, right? You're just fantasizing about it, aren't you? I don't know, Sonia, but I find it weird that everywhere we go, you talk about moving there. And all those books about the Midwest and shit. It bothers me. I'm happy where we are."

"I don't know if I'm happy where we are. I guess I feel trapped. In Brooklyn. Maybe I should go away for the weekend. Alone."

"Great idea."

"Or for a week."

"That would be a little harder to swing, but we could try and make it work."

"Oh yeah?" And Sonia thinks, this is what this is all about. I don't want to move my whole family to the Poconos. I don't want to move my whole family to New Jersey. I want to go away. I want to flee. And I can't admit it. I'm afraid I'll actually do it. And so, I pretend I want to move to Bayfield, Wisconsin. Sonia looks at Dick. His kind, droopy face surrounded by thinning brown hair. His stern expression that hides the fact that he's a pervert and a freak, like everyone else. He's like Clara that way, really. Looks one way, *is* another. And Sonia thinks, I love him but I feel, if I have to look at this face every day for the rest of my life, that I may jump off a building. And then she looks out to where her children play by the water, sticks in hands. And she thinks, Tom and Mike, if someone else served them breakfast, lunch and dinner, they'd be fine. I could jump off that building. I could go. They'd continue on without me. And then the panic comes and her head begins to shake. She runs to the boys and they look toward her, their mother, and they notice the fear in her face and they stop what they are playing. They stand frozen, as she comes to them and falls to her knees, her arms outstretched.

11

It's deep November and Sonia goes maternity clothes shopping with Clara. They both hire babysitters for the event. They take the train into the city together and have lunch at the South Street Seaport before heading over to Mimi Maternity in the World Trade Center Mall. There's a slight distance between the two women and Sonia remembers that Clara thinks pregnant women are disgusting. When Clara was pregnant, she referred to her belly as the "costume". As soon as she gave birth, she joked about it. "Finally got rid of the costume," she'd say, laughing.

Sonia is feeling doughy and uninspired. Shopping isn't her thing. It's just a chore, something that has to be done. There is no pleasure in it. Her blond hair is dry and the dye isn't holding well. Her somewhat trashy look is exaggerated by her weight and slovenly hair. Whereas once Sonia was chic trashy, now she seems ready to move into a trailer, back to the Midwest, from whence she came. At lunch, Sonia devours a greasy cheeseburger. Ketchup smears on her chin, her finger wet and drippy.

"You know, you could use your napkin," Clara says, unable to hide her disgust as she takes a bite of her salad.

"God, I'm so starved all the time," Sonia says. "It's great not to feel sick anymore. But I'm insatiable."

"I can see that."

"All I want to do is eat and fuck, eat and fuck. Did that happen to you when you were pregnant?" Clara shakes her head at Sonia, who continues, "But I don't want Dick to fuck me. It's strange. This happened with my last two pregnancies, too. I was desperate for sex, but I wouldn't let Dick touch me after a while."

Clara puts a small forkful of green leaves into her mouth. "So who do you want to fuck?"

"I don't know. The bathtub spout? My vibrator?"

"You mean you want to masturbate."

"I don't know what I want. Every time I'm pregnant, I feel like I'm on the edge of a cliff. You know? Or that I want to be on the edge of a cliff. Maybe I should call my shrink."

"Well, to be honest with you, Sonia, I have totally blacked out my pregnancies. It's like I never was pregnant, really. It's like it happened to someone else. They say we biologically forget the pain of childbirth so that we'll do it again. You know, the propagation of the species. But I've also managed, thankfully, to forget my pregnancies. I know that I was pregnant—twice, in fact—but that's all I can tell you."

"I'm having panic attacks."

"Really?"

"Yeah, big bad ones."

"What's that like?"

"It's sort of like an acid flashback."

"You'll have to explain that one to me."

"Well, everything around me becomes unreal and I just want to flee. A fear and flight response occurs in the body. It's supposed to happen, for instance, if a bear approaches you. It's a normal response if the body is under attack. It becomes a disorder if you get one, say, while you are grocery shopping. Which is happening to me."

"Wow, that sucks, Sonia. Maybe you should see your shrink." Sonia knows that Clara thinks seeing a therapist is pathetic. They've discussed this before. Personally, Sonia thinks—suspects and thinks and almost *hopes*, because Clara has been getting on her nerves lately, and wouldn't it be a trip—that it's because Clara is gay and doesn't want to deal with the fact of her gayness, as it would royally fuck up the whole lifestyle she's got going. "Maybe I will see him. But I know what you think of shrinks, Clara. Funny you should mention it."

"Well, I mean, yeah. I think if you have problems, you're better off joining the Marines or something. But you can't do that pregnant. I don't know. I mean I would never see a shrink, but you're not me."

Sonia looks at her friend and does all she can to not say *just be GAY. It's the twenty-first century, just be GAY.* "Yeah, he's been helpful in the past. And I'm suffering."

"Let's get a bunch of pretty pink baby clothes and some clothes that fit you and maybe that will cheer you up."

"Thanks for coming with me, Clara. You know I'm not much of a shopper."

"Of course! I love shopping. I could be a professional shopper."

"Good. I'll just follow you around and say yes to stuff."

"Sounds perfect." Clara grins at her and Sonia feels OK, almost OK, even if behind that OKness lurks the panic, waiting for its moment to pounce.

THAT NIGHT, AFTER SONIA cooks a chicken for her family and Dick helps her clean up, after the kids are tucked in their beds and Dick is in front of the TV, Sonia unpacks her carefully wrapped maternity clothes up in their loft. There is the pair of khaki pants with a huge elastic stomach that Clara convinced her she had to buy. There is a pair of pants that resembles the black sweats Sonia wore every day until they stopped fitting her. There's two black T-shirts, a blue T-shirt and a white one, all cut for a burgeoning belly. And there is the most dreadful thing of all, maternity underpants. As Sonia unpacks these items and holds them up in front of her face, the TV making a slight noise from down below, her hands begin to shake. She's holding the blue shirt, the one Clara told her she had to have, and it seems enormous, it seems like it's mocking her, and her hands go cold as if her blood just froze. The shirt jitters in her hands in front of her and Sonia puts it down. How did she survive this before? And then again? Those two children were wanted, they were, despite her nagging doubts and fears. This time, it's totally different. She never wanted three children. With three children, you can't fit in the booth. With three children, you can't fit in a station wagon, you need a minivan. With three children, you are outnumbered. You have to learn how to play zone defense. With three children—and it hits her, it's a sharp stab straight in her brain, it's a revelation, it's like finding Christ—there won't be anything left of herself. She'll be eaten alive. She'll disappear. Now her head starts swarming and her hands, as she holds them up to her face, look red. They *are* red. They start to ooze sweat, her palms glisten as she turns her hands around in front of her face. They burn with heat, this, just after rattling with ice. It's the start of an anxiety attack and Sonia knows it, but it doesn't make it OK. She feels as if she's going to faint and she throws herself down on the bed, shaking, breathing rapidly, and she buries her face in pile of enormous underwear and cries without a sound. She can't do this. She's made a mistake. She needs to call her shrink.

⁓

THE NEXT MORNING, DICK takes the kids to school. "Are you OK, sweetie?" Sonia looks ashen. Pregnancies can have complications, she knows from their various friends. They were lucky with their two boys in that although Sonia was a psycho-bitch when she was pregnant, she didn't get high blood pressure, she didn't get diabetes, she didn't get any of the bad things that one can get when one is pregnant. But now Dick looks worried because Sonia looks horrible.

"I think I've seen a ghost," she says, and she thinks, *I've seen the ghost of my future.*

"Call Dr. Silver, Sonia. And maybe go see your midwife and get your blood pressure and stuff checked." He sits on the bed next to her. Sonia looks at him, but does not see him.

"Yeah, maybe I'll call Dr. Silver," she says, and they kiss goodbye, lightly, and the boys run up to her and throw themselves at her and everyone gets kisses and goodbyes and she lays there and thinks, *I'm not calling my shrink.*

I'm not calling my shrink because he can't make me not be pregnant. I'm not calling my shrink because I don't want someone watching over me, trying to get me to get through my days like a good person. Like a responsible person. I don't want to cook dinner for anyone, I don't want to do laundry, I don't want to pick up milk. I don't want to be that well-functioning person that everyone wants me to be. I want out. I want out of here. And my shrink won't "support" me on that. My shrink's on their side, even if he pretends to be working for me.

The apartment is quiet. She pulls herself out of bed and she's not shaking. She's calm. This pleases her and she hums while she showers and afterward, after rubbing herself dry delicately so that it feels really nice, her flesh all damp and clean and the towel kissing her, then, then, she pulls on her new maternity black sweatpants. They are big and make her look and feel like a cow but hey, she doesn't fit into anything else so what else is she to do? And she's still relatively small, considering how far along she is. Then she attempts to put on her new blue maternity shirt and that's it, her calmness is gone. Her rage has been triggered. The fucking shirt, the pale blue huge shirt. It is not what she is. She rips it off and scrapes her ear in the process and pulls on a Hanes wife-beater and then grabs her old black leather jacket from the closet, and dammit, she's shaking again. Her apartment seems tilted sideways as she stands in the center of it. It's a lovely apartment. Dick picked up all of the toys. The floor shines up at her, the dark brown wood serene and perfect in front of her. This is her home. She's always loved this apartment but it's too small for three kids. Exposed brick walls, the large open living room with a soaring ceiling. The loft, the privacy of the loft, their bedroom. The children's room off the small kitchen. They'd had such a good life here. But she doesn't belong here.

She doesn't call Dr. Silver. She doesn't even call her husband. She calls Clara, who answers the phone.

"Hello?"

"Clara?"

"Hi, Sonia! Wearing that blue maternity shirt I told you to get? It was the best color for you. It matched your eyes perfectly."

"Clara, I have to ask you a favor."

"Sure thing."

"I need you to pick up the boys from school today."

"OK." Says Clara. "Are you OK? Is everything OK?"

"Everything is not OK. Oh, and after you pick them up, call Dick at work, OK? His number is 212-652-7742. Got that?"

"What's going on Sonia. Are you OK? Are you going to the hospital?" Clara asks.

"I'm not going to the hospital. Don't worry. Thanks for doing this for me," Sonia says.

Clara can tell she's about to hang up. "Wait, Sonia. Don't go. What's going on? You have to tell me."

"Thanks a lot, Clara. I gotta go." And that's it. She hangs up. She throws her new maternity clothes in a bag and heads out the door.

As she walks to the garage to get the car, her legs feel like rotten vegetables, like mushy stalks of zucchini. Will they live without her? And she didn't even say goodbye.

How can they live without her? If she's not there, she will be dead to them. They took away her life, they didn't mean to, but they did. And now here she goes, pretending she can claim it back.

AND AS SHE STARTS up the car, she thinks, where am I going? And then she thinks, it doesn't matter. I'm going, I'm gone, I'm doing what every mother dreams of doing because I've always followed my dreams. I'm doing what every mother fears she'll do, because I've always confronted my fears. I'm doing something really terrible and I'll be punished for it, no doubt, but I've always been a trouble-maker. And that's it, her hands want to shake but they can't shake too much because she's driving. They want to freeze but she grips the wheel and it keeps them warm. And her mind starts to expand and then it stops, because she has to focus on the road. It's called survival. Fear and flight. Our natural reaction to a bear in the woods. Sonia's been in the woods. And the bear's her whole fucking life.

12

Once Sonia gets going on 95 going north, once she is definitely out of the city, it is all she can do not to slam on the breaks and turn back, or slam on the gas pedal and speed 100 miles an hour. She feels . . . *extreme*. She's free! Every now and then she lets out a high-pitched squeal of delight and fear. But it is the beginning of her trip, of her adventure—indeed, the very first day—and so she's not comfortable really talking or exclaiming out loud to herself. (That would come later.) Hence, the high-pitchedness of her squeal. Things had not gotten gutteral. Not yet.

As the day wears on and she drives further and further into the New England countryside, past the suburbs, deep into the hilly, tree-laden world that is Massachusetts, she's struck with how gorgeous the world really is. The sun hangs deep and yellow in the painfully clear sky, the trees sparkle every shade of orange and red. Autumn in the country. And she's alone! Alone at last! No crying babies demanding she try to stick a bottle in their mouths while driving. No toddlers saying, "I'm bored. Are we there yet?" No young child throwing up from carsickness. No one demanding to stop because they have to pee so badly they are about to wet their car seat.

Except that Sonia has to pee. And even if there are no children in the car—she glances into the rearview mirror just to make sure—*nope, no children!*—there are the car seats, accusingly empty.

The miles accumulate. Traffic is sparse. The sun is setting and a darkness settles in. She turns on the lights and the road spreads out gray and weakly lit before her. Funny how lights on a car don't feel important until it's deep into the night. She's been listening to CDs and, alternately, to the radio, and now her ears hurt. She turns down the music. A green sign saying rest stop in three miles presents itself. *Good*, she thinks. She can make it until there.

And she does. But barely. She parks the Passat as near to the restrooms as she can and then rushes into the bathroom, whose smell reminds her of a pig farm she drove by on a family road trip combined with a dead rat she removed from the courtyard of an old apartment—a juicy, rotten stink. She sits on the toilet seat without thinking or looking and, immediately, her ass feels wet. Her wet, cold butt sticking to the toilet seat fuels the cancerous growth of self-hatred that Sonia has festering inside of her. She is disgusting and incompetent. But she is peeing and feels some relief. And it dawns on her that this is the first of many public bathrooms she will encounter.

Afterward, she manages a decent cleanup job. There is toilet paper—hallelujah!—and even warm water in the sinks. She stares at herself in the mirror. She sticks her chest out. She has the *glow*. The pregnancy glow. The moist skin, the seemingly smiling face. The Mona Lisa smile that all pregnant women get. It's not a real smile, but it seems like one to the outside world. She sticks her tongue out and leaves the restroom.

It is a beautiful night. Even here, next to the highway. The air is crisp and cool and her nipples harden under her tank top. And even though cars whiz by on the highway occasionally, the rhythmic noises of crickets and birds overwhelm the traffic. Sonia sits on top of her car, delicately though, as it feels a bit warm. She folds her hands in her lap and breathes slowly for a minute, her eyes closed. *I'm here now*, she thinks, *that's all. Nothing else matters.*

There are a handful of other cars. A few spots away from her Passat, with no cars in between, is a green Chevy pickup, with a young, dark-haired man leaning against it, holding a cup of coffee and smoking a cigarette.

Sonia immediately likes him. His dirty hair, long but not too long, like a haircut gone neglected. His pants are tight, but not painfully so. He's got tattoos, which she notices first. Then she notices his arms. They are *big*.

"You're staring at me."

"I'm sorry?" Sonia calls back.

"You're staring at me." In the low light, it's hard to see if he's smiling, what his expression is.

"Can I bum a cigarette?"

Sonia hasn't smoked since college. She walks over and every muscle in her body feels tight and strange, as if walking were something her body had never done before. He taps out a Camel filter for her. He looks older than he is. He has that reddish-tan seeming skin that has a bit to do with the sun, and much to do with cigarettes and alcohol. Sonia finds it sexy in him—decadent, reckless.

"I haven't had a cigarette in a long time," she says.

"Are you pregnant?"

Sonia looks down at her bump. She feigns surprise. "Look! I am pregnant!"

"Phew. For a minute there, I thought I had made a mistake." He has an accent that Sonia can't place. "That's no good, saying a woman looks pregnant when she's not." He laughs, looking away from her.

But quickly, he's leaning toward her, flicking his lighter at the cigarette in her mouth. She doesn't inhale, but she holds the dry smoke in her mouth. It's too much. Her hand shakes as she takes the cigarette out from between her lips.

"Where are you from?" she asks him.

"From Hingham, the south shore of Boston. I was visiting my dad. He lives in Connecticut. Where are you from?"

"From Brooklyn," she answers, and then wonders if this is the time where she starts lying about where's she's from. Or if she's pregnant. Let them think she's fat! Who cares? Guys fuck fat chicks. Some guys do. Or if she's married. The hand with the cigarette, her left hand, sports a wedding ring. She wonders if she should take it off. Hell, guys fuck married women all the time. In fact, Sonia decides, many may prefer to. Perhaps the sort of man Sonia is looking for prefers married women. If Sonia is looking for men, which she's not quite sure about. Is she looking for *men*? For what? For laughs? She is looking at this man now. He is beautiful to her. The cigarette and his arms and his accent and everything about him, his truck everything, is making her feel weak, lightheaded.

"Where're you heading?" he asks.

"That's a good question. I guess to Boston. I'm on a road trip. And I don't have a strict itinerary."

He smells good. She's standing so close to him that she can really smell him. He smells salty and smoky. Like he's been sweating a bit, but not too much. His biceps bulge, his tattoo is of a dragon, his arms are covered with coarse, dark hair.

"Are you OK?" he asks and he puts a hand on her arm.

"Yeah, the cigarette just made me dizzy." But really, it's

his touch that pushes her over the edge. "Can I sit in your truck for a minute?"

Now he looks at her strangely.

"Please?" she says, weakly.

"Sure." She can hear a bit of nervousness in his voice. "I do have to be going soon." He starts looking around himself, as if he was waiting for someone.

She wants to scream, Fuck You! Pussy! What are you afraid of? Be a Man! Help Me Out! But instead, she says, "Thanks. Just for a minute."

Then she looks at his face. He's chiseled. It's as if she ran into Colin Farrell here on the side of 95 in deep New England. Except this guy's taller, and smells. And he probably gets his cut arms from doing real work, not from hanging out with his personal trainer. God how Sonia hates actors, the whole concept of them, pretending to be real people. But she *loves* men. She loves real men.

"Come sit next to me." Her voice comes out smooth, a little deep.

"Are you married?" He's standing in the doorway of the driver's seat, she's already scooted over the bench—this truck has a bench!—to the passenger's side. He's got one leg crossed over the other.

"Not really. My husband . . . my husband died. Just sit next to me." Oh, boy, thinks Sonia, this guy is young. All the cigarettes and booze in the world can't kill this hard, strong youthfulness underneath. Good lord, he could be nineteen.

"Wow." He sits next to her. "Is he the father of your child?"

"Shh." She puts a finger up to his lips and looks into his eyes, leaning a bit closer. He wants it, too. Or so she hopes. Prays. *Dear God, please let this guy want to fuck me.* "Don't talk about it. I'm not so pregnant yet," she says, rubbing her hands gently on her smooth, rounded belly. "I'm still toward the beginning. Not yet the middle. But feel this," she says and takes his hand—God, the feel of his hand, so rough, this man is a *laborer*—and places it firmly on her right breast.

He looks away, out the back window. With his free hand he slams the truck door shut. It's dark out now.

She reaches out to his face and she's kissing him. He tastes sour, stale and dry. She's nervous but she keeps at it and he's kissing her and squeezing her breast. She lifts up her tank top and pulls up her bra over her breasts and takes both of his hands and puts them on her tits. Oh, *God!* This is so *wrong!* Now his mouth goes down on them and she moans—her nipples are so hot and painful, she almost comes just from his mouth on them, she's bucking her hips up toward him now.

Suddenly, he pulls back. "I can't do this," he says quietly. Then he grabs her breasts again and she sits on top of him and grinds against his erection. His dick is *big*. Everything about this guy is huge. His big arms are around her body now, now her neck, on her side. She hoists herself up and starts the awkward undressing, the ripping, the *just a min-ute*, the *I got it, I got it*, the *wait, not yet.*

First she's on top and he's inside of her, but she can barely get him all in there. Then he pushes her down on the bench, she stretches one of her legs over the car seat and *wham*. He's fucking her. It hurts some, in that good way that fucking hurts. She hates to look in the eyes of Dick when she's fucking him, but for some reason, here in the dark with this stranger, she looks straight at him. His eyes glow like cat's eyes in the dark. His mouth is loose and open. He looks right back at her and then spits on his thumb and puts it on the base of her clit and pushes very, very gently. This man knows pussy. He fucks her hard, his other free hand on her hipbone and her breasts start shak-ing in her face and she comes, the vision of it all, the sor-didness, the feel of it. It's so awful. It's so right. God. God! To get fucked in a truck on the side of a highway by a man who doesn't give a shit about her, about what's for dinner, about their social life, about, about . . . how the kids are today. And when he's about to come, she screams, "Don't take it out! I can't get pregnant! I am pregnant! Don't pull out! Come, *come inside me!*"

Which he does.

AFTER, SHE WASHES UP in the bathroom again—she wipes the seat carefully this time—and when she comes back out, his truck is gone. Which is all fine and well. She heads toward the Passat. She opens the backseat doors and one by one, throws her sons' car seats on the grass. She grabs her cellphone out of her purse and tosses it in the garbage can. Then she gets back in the car and drives, drives on, she sings to herself, deeply now, her voice coming out without that squeal, in her car without children's car seats and maybe she is free, really free, for the first time in a very, very long time.

13

What does it mean to have no plans? To be on the lam? Sonia stops at a branch of her bank in Connecticut. She withdraws everything in the savings account. Seven thousand dollars. Then she keeps driving. It's dark, she's not a great driver in the dark, that's what living in New York City does to you, but she has a feeling she's about to get better at it.

She checks into a hotel, a cheap Holiday Inn Express in Brighton, on the outskirts of Boston. Brighton still had a sort of Irish and immigrant vibe to it when Sonia lived in Boston, all those years ago, when she was actually free, free because she was young and had no real responsibilities, not free as she was now, because she was abandoning very real responsibilities. Ironically, when she was actually free, it felt just like life, not like freedom. But now that she was stealing it, it felt exhilarating and much more real and visceral. She felt it, coursing through her body.

Nineteen. At first, she hadn't been very good at being young. She was too earnest, too serious. She read anti-pornography feminist tracts and existential philosophy. She painted dark, morbid figures, writhing in pain and blood. Then she met Katrina. Katrina changed her life.

Katrina. Beautiful, fabulous, irresistible Katrina—men were sucked down into Katrina as if she were some wild, inescapable drain. And yet, she had a big nose, occasional acne, tiny breasts, and she was barely 5'4". How? Katrina, who had painted swirly, psychedelic things. Elaborate six-ties druggy paintings while listening to scratched-up Robert Johnson records. Katrina, who taught Sonia that being female wasn't weak. The woman—girl, really, they had only been nineteen, the both of them—that taught Sonia that lying on your back with your legs spread open was a kind of power, especially if it felt really good. The one that taught Sonia how to wear a short skirt, how to shake her ass when she walked in said skirt, and how to turn every eye in the room, even if you don't have tits, because Katrina didn't have tits, either. What was it about her? Fearless-ness. Confidence. She used to say to Sonia, "You are only going to be nineteen once in your life. Just once. Why not enjoy it? Why not really make the most of youth and freedom?" And she was right. She was so fucking right. Prior to meeting Katrina, she threw herself at her painting with a humorless dedication. After meeting Katrina, her whole relationship to life, and to art, changed. After meeting Katrina, she started getting seriously laid. She started fucking with abandon. Whomever she wanted. Little art boys with their hairless faces and permanently hard cocks. Rock drummers were a specialty for a while, too. And her instructors, oh yes, her instructors. Particularly Philbert Rush. Tall, startling dark hair sticking up on the sides of his head like a cartoon of a mad scientist, handsome largely due to his arrogance, not any conventional good looks, a great deal older, thin and grumpy. Loved pussy in a way no twenty-year-old can. Katrina had no time for older men, but Sonia had time for all sorts of men. Yes, Sonia started to enjoy herself, really truly and wildly, enjoy herself for the first time in her life. And had that been the last? Was that it? Had Sonia peaked in college, like some girls—cheerleader types—peaked in high school?

Sonia met Katrina while working at an Italian restaurant on Newbury Street. It was a decent job in some respects. The money was good, the work wasn't so horrible, though the man who owned the restaurant was completely crazy. He cooked, too, and his wife helped on weekends, and often they fought so horrifically—screaming and throwing pots and pans, and really, really screaming—that Katrina and Sonia would have to turn up the radio very loudly so as not to freak out the customers. They would smile at each other when this happened. It was the conversation opener between the two of them. Because Katrina didn't like Sonia at first. Sonia knew that. Katrina didn't like "college" girls. Katrina didn't go to school. She went to rock shows. But Sonia had been insistent. And funny, without trying to be so. Katrina laughed at her, not with her, but that was OK with Sonia. At least she wasn't being totally ignored anymore. And Sonia was just so intrigued. Who was this woman, this mildly weird-looking woman, who thought so highly of herself? Who sashayed around the restaurant like everyone should lick her toes?

After work, Sonia would go home and dream restlessly of waiting on tables. The next morning, she'd wake tired, her neck and arms hurting from carrying trays of food. She was often too tired to paint in the mornings. One night she asked Katrina if she had the dreams, too.

"They're called waitressing nightmares," Katrina said. "Dreams isn't the right word."

"And you're always carrying food and can never get it to the customer?"

"You can never find your table. It's waitressing hell in your sleep. Waitressing is haunting work. I've been doing it for three years."

"Here? Three years here?" Sonia had just started a few months ago, right before the spring semester ended.

"No, you crazy college girl." Katrina laughed at Sonia. But it was all right. Sonia didn't mind amusing Katrina. Because honestly, her attraction to Katrina was piqued by a curiosity that was somewhat objectifying. Everyone Sonia knew was at a college. Beyond not going to college, Katrina hadn't even finished high school, and Sonia had never hung out with a high school dropout before. "What do they teach you in that fancy school? That people often work at the same place for three years?"

"Well I'm sure it has happened before. And I study painting, not the work habits of the American people."

Katrina smiled at her. Again, it was a bemused smile, not completely friendly. At this point, Sonia hadn't yet understood the magic that was Katrina. She looked at Katrina and she saw a shaggy-haired, wide-bottomed short girl with a long nose who didn't go to college. Katrina said, "Do you want to go out with me after work? I'm going to the Paradise to see a band. This bass player I know put me on the list plus one. My sister was going to be my plus one, but she can get in by herself. She knows the guy at the door. Rock 'n' roll is a great way to make sure you don't get the waitressing nightmares. It clears the head of all waitressing things before sleep. You'll dream of other things, I promise."

And so it went. Free drinks, backstage passes. Small-time bands and then the bigger ones, visiting from LA, from New York, from Chicago. There was Lemmy from Motörhead. There were endless hair bands. Katrina got banged by everyone, by Slash, the guy from Warrant, Chris Robinson from the Black Crowes, Tommy from

the Replacements, the guitar player from the Chili Pep-
pers. Katrina knew everybody, cool or uncool. Sonia never
had a waitressing nightmare again. Granted, she got stuck
with whomever Katrina didn't want. But that was fine with
her. Because it was all experience. They were all people.
Well, men actually. And it was all fun. Lighthearted. It
was adrenaline rushes and loud-ass music and sweaty men
and drugs and alcohol. It was short skirts and tight shirts
and the power of a well-shaped nipple. A nineteen-year-
old nipple. What was more beautiful than a pink, swollen
nineteen year old girl's nipple? Nothing. Absolutely nothing. And Sonia learned that there was no shame in that,
only joy. Only joy in the beauty of youth, if you were brave
enough to feel it.

But that was years ago. Over ten years ago. Fucking
fifteen years ago. Now, Sonia's nipples, well, they weren't
outrageously bad, but they were darker, not as pink, a
little wider. She turns on the TV in her sterile Holiday
Inn Express room. She flips through the channels. She lies
down and it feels good to put her feet up, After an hour or
so of resting like that, she begins to feel restless, hungry,
a little alarmed at herself. She even calls home and Dick
answers and she hangs up. He was alive. They were all
alive. They. And then she calls information in Boston, and
then the greater Boston area, and then she finds her, with a
hyphenated last name, Katrina Nelson-Allen, in Harvard,

Massachusetts. But she chickens out and doesn't call her. Instead, she puts on the one dress she brought, a babydoll dress from years ago, from Betsy Johnson, when babydoll dresses were fashionable among rock chicks, and it works when she's pregnant, making her look not so pregnant, and her swelling breasts hang out the top nicely, all cleavagey. She leaves her hotel, getting the desk guy to call her a cab and decides to go the Kenmore Square, to go to the Rat, her favorite club from her years in Boston, the best fucking rock club in the world.

The Rat. Where she danced to the Pixies, the Neighborhoods, the Bags, Ultra Blue, Jawbreaker and, well, a hundred other bands. Mitch had worked the door, Mitch who had a hole in his throat and this little microphone thing he put up to it when he wanted to talk. Not that he talked much to Katrina and Sonia, as they sashayed by him, letting him feel their asses, not asking for the cover charge. Mitch was a huge man and had tons of gray hair and a gray beard and he really was an institution, he was in charge, he could bounce out anyone, the Del Fuegos when they got too drunk, frat boys who weren't regulars but were trying to slum it and he just didn't like. He had *power*. Rock 'n' Roll power. And he loved Katrina and Sonia, because what was not to love about them?

The cab stops in front of the Rat, which looks exactly the same and this delights Sonia beyond all belief, as if the world was truly wonderful and made for her happiness.

She puts on some lipstick, checks her face in her compact, and then as she walks toward the Rat, feeling self-conscious of being pregnant—although, man, she's really carrying so nice and small, but pregnant is pregnant—notices something is wrong. There's a big football-player-looking guy at the door, all steroid muscles and tight shirt with a leather jacket and spiked hair.

Sonia walks sort of slowly up to him, peaks in behind him. The bar looks the same. It's crowded, but not too crowded, loud, louder than she's used to these days but probably not louder than it was back in her day. But where's Mitch? A sort of panic sets in.

"Hi," Sonia says.

"Hi," football player says, with a reassuring Boston accent. "The cover's ten bucks."

"Oh, of course." Sonia reaches in her bag, finds a ten in her wallet. She can't believe she's paying a cover charge. Her face goes red. "You know, I never had to pay a cover here before. Where's Mitch? Mitch . . . well, Mitch . . . "

"Mitch is dead."

Sonia swayed, put her hand on the door to steady herself. "What? Mitch is dead?"

"Yeah, the throat cancer came back and killed him." Stunned, Sonia barely notices the guy take her ten dollars, her anger overwhelmed by grief. Mitch was dead. Mitch, who made her feel special, like she was in the club of hot girls who got to bang hot rock boys. Mitch, Mob

connected, the man who put up with nothing, who pro-
tected all the girls he loved. Sonia remembers the time he
beat up Ike Wagner, a local rock hero, because he tried
to rape some poor girl in the men's room. And he beat
the shit out of him, movie-style blood and action, right in
front of the Rat. Wagner would never press charges, not
with Mitch's connections. He was a hero, a legend.

She gathers herself, walks first to the upstairs bar, rather
than going down in the basement where the bands play.
She sits up on a barstool and gets the attention of the the
bartender and orders a beer and a burger. He brings her
the beer and she catches his eye.

"So when did Mitch die?" she asks.

"Mitch? Who's Mitch?"

"Oh boy, forget it." This makes her feel even worse. It's
one thing for Mitch to be dead, it was a whole other thing
when someone working at the Rat doesn't even know who
he was. It was like not knowing who Jesus was or something.

Sonia, stunned and quiet, spaces out until her burger
arrives, and arrives it does. Greasy, huge, hitting the spot.
Sonia sips her beer and manages a moment of being super
grateful to be eating large quantities of food. Then, a man
sits next to her, and she's midbite—a big-ass bite—when
he says, "Hi, Sonia. Jeez, long time no see," and he goes
in for a hug. Sonia worries she might dribble on him so
she doesn't say anything, just makes a muffled sound, and

doesn't pull away from the hug, because, well, it must be someone she knows.

And it is, but it takes her a while to recognize him. Because it appears life has not been kind to him. It was Katrina's boyfriend, the one she lived with for a year, the bass player for many bands, most notably the Neighborhoods. Stan. Stan Donato. His hair is still mostly black and still cut in the same shag haircut. He'd always been thin, but now he's rail thin, and his skin—his face—good Lord. Not that he ever had good skin, but wow, he has not aged well. He's positively gray and although he'd never been a tall man, he now seems shrunken, like half the size he had been. And yet, it's great to see him.

"Stan! It's good to see you. What a surprise," Sonia manages after swallowing some burger.

"You're the surprise, Sonia. What are you doing in Boston?" Stan croaks, like an old man.

"I'm not sure what I'm doing here."

"You look great." He looks down at her stomach.

"I'm pregnant."

"Wow. Congratulations."

"Thanks."

"Are you married? I think I heard you were married."

"Yeah. I am." Sonia clears her throat from burger. "Tell me about yourself while I wolf the rest of this burger down."

"Oh same old, same old, but all good. I'm playing bass

with this really great new band. I think we could be huge. We got some labels interested but we might go the DIY way, just put out an album." Stan scratches his face in an elaborate and familiar way. He's jonesing for a fix. Sonia recognizes the particular way of face scratching heroin addicts have. "I'm still living in the same apartment in Allston. I got a great new girl, she's awesome. So much better for me than Katrina was. Are you in touch with Katrina?"

"No, no I'm not. I looked her up, thought about calling her."

"I wouldn't bother, she's married with a kid and goes to AA and is like totally a different person. Although personally I always knew she was a bitch. I just loved her anyway."

"I wouldn't call her a bitch. She had a lot of attitude but that was something you liked about her. Wow, though. To think of her settled down. I find that, hard. Maybe disconcerting."

"You have no idea, Sonia," says Stan. "I visited her a few times because we stayed friends."

"I remember that now. I was always amazed. I've never stayed friends with any of my exes." Dick flashes into Sonia's mind but she quickly refocuses.

Sonia thinks of Katrina walking off with Lenny Kravitz in a smoke-filled club, or dancing, arms outstretched to the Black Crowes. "Well, I looked her up and wussed out on calling her. But I think I will. I'd like to see her even if

she's into AA. I'm married with kids. But I don't feel like
a different person. Maybe that's the problem. I feel like I
have different things to do now, but otherwise, I feel the
same, I think." As Sonia says this, looking over Stan, who
was the same, just a fifteen-years-older version, which
wasn't pretty, she wonders if it's true, if she does feel the
same. And what does that mean anyway? Young? Free?
As if the whole world lay ahead of her?

"Is your whole family here? What are you doing here,
did you say?" Stan scratches away, dragging his fingers
down his face, from his forehead to his chin and back again.

"I didn't say. I . . . I guess I'm on a vacation. Or on a mission. A find-myself mission. I don't know. But no, my family
is not with me."

"Where are you staying?"

"At a Holiday Inn Express in Brighton." Sonia is done
eating. "Hey, should we go check out the bands below?"

Stan shrugs. Sonia can tell he's just looking to score, but
she can also tell he needs money to do so.

"Let's just check them out."

The band is called Let's Go Radio! and really does have
an exclamation point in the name. They seem to be imitat-
ing bands from the '80s, bands that she had grown up listening to, like Men Without Hats and Flock of Seagulls, but
their look is less colorful. Sonia and Stan stand in the back,
and Sonia eyes the young girls, with tons of eyeliner and
bright tights, jumping around, wagging their asses, hands

grasping the edge of the stage. That had been her. Shame-less. But why not have been shameless? Why not, when so young? The real problem right now is she hates this band. They suck. It's as if they didn't even tune their instruments. And something about being here felt wrong, like she's star-ing into her past and missing it and yet this is not her past, this is now and it's not nearly as haloed as her past was. Not to mention there's no going back. And then she turns and looks at Stan and thinks, at least I'm not in the same apart-ment, fifteen years later, still trying to make it and, worse, a junkie to boot.

"Let's get out of here," Stan says. "These guys suck."

"I know, they really do."

They walk down Commonwealth Avenue, and Stan shares the news of some of her ex-boyfriends—one in San Francisco making art rock, another disappeared in New Hampshire with a waitress and no one knows where he is. A bench presents itself. The night feels nice, airy and cool, but comfortable. They sit.

"So listen, Sonia, I have a favor to ask you."

She knew this was coming. Stan drags his fingers down his face again, his body twitching in a way that reminds her of Mike, her toddler, trying to sit still and then she banishes the thought of Mike and looks at Stan.

"Can I borrow sixteen dollars?"

What was it with junkies? They always came up with the strangest amounts of money to ask for. I mean, not a hundred bucks or something round and significant, it was always some weird specific amount, the amount of half a bag, because they had the rest in their pocket or something? Who knew.

"Stan, I . . ."

"I can pay you back next week. We've got a gig and I'll get paid and I can . . . I can send you a check." He looks straight at her, wringing his hands.

"Stan, since when do you have a checking account?"

"How about fourteen dollars? Or fourteen fifty? I'm begging you."

"You're just gonna buy drugs and I don't feel right about that."

"No, no!" Stan's eyes widen in an enormous effort at sincerity. Sonia knows drug addiction isn't funny, but watching his face attempt to form itself into some wide-eyed semblance of innocence is making it hard for her not to laugh. "I just need it to, to, get home and buy some dinner. I'm just broke! And I owe some money. I need to pay back a . . . a friend."

"Stan, no. You know, it's been so great running into you. Hearing even a bit about Katrina, about my exes. It was really great to see you, but I'm going to catch a cab back to my hotel." Sonia leans in and hugs him. And he hugs her back. He doesn't even smell that bad. They pull apart and she stands to find a cab.

"Sonia, wait, Sonia." Stan remains sitting, desperate.

She feels for him but no, she's always had a rule about junkies. Junk was just so nasty.

"Yeah, Stan?"

He grabs her hands and pulls her head to his and says, "I'll give you head. I give great head. Just fourteen dollars. . . . "

Sonia pulls away and starts waving, "Oh no, no, Stan. Take care, man. I mean, thanks, but no." She starts walking as fast as she can and turns and waves at Stan, who sits slumped on the bench, waving half-heartedly back at her.

BACK IN THE HOTEL, Sonia contemplates calling home, if she's allowed to call it that, and hanging up, but thinks better of it. Katrina, dear Katrina. The thing is, nothing about Katrina could ever really surprise her. She was capable of anything, going in any direction. And Stan, oh boy. He was so hugely talented and now look. Exhausted, even as her mind races, she turns on the television and before she knows it, she's falling asleep so she gets up, rips off her clothes and begins passing out, inhaling the clean bleach smell of hotel sheets and right before she loses consciousness, her last thought is an ache for the warm, dirty flesh smell of her bed.

14

"Katrina? This is Sonia. I know we haven't talked in years . . ." Sonia did it. She called her and it was wonderful to hear her voice. Just wonderful.

And it's settled. Sonia would visit. Sonia didn't say anything about leaving her family. From their quick conversation she knows that Katrina has a little boy, Rufus. Her husband, Joe, had been in one of the local Boston bands, surely Sonia remembers him? Actually, Sonia doesn't, but will when she sees him. She's good with faces, bad with names. And Sonia doesn't remember too many details from their groupie days. She remembers a wash of emotion and noise and color. But the fine lines, for the most part, were gone to her. Not that she doesn't want to try to remember. Maybe seeing Katrina would bring back the specifics. Maybe what Sonia needs is to truly remember her life.

———

KATRINA'S HOUSE IS BEAUTIFUL on the outside. Gray clap-
board. Like a house on the Cape. Sprawling, with white
shutters. The grass is mowed. The gravel driveway tasteful
and not too bumpy.

And then here comes Katrina, coming out to greet her
as she pulls in the drive. She has Rufus on her hip and he
seems to be nearly the size of her. She looks beautiful, her
hair longer and shaggier than ever, with a thick block of
heavy bangs covering her forehead. She is thin and hippy,
her face so youthful that Sonia immediately feels old as
shit. Sonia feels that her taste for booze and cigarettes,
although greatly curtailed during this pregnancy and her
other pregnancies, has aged her, and for some reason,
Katrina, walking toward her with this scowling, enormous
boy wrapped around her, is dewy-skinned. They hug awkwardly, Rufus and Sonia's belly both interfering with the
hug and then they walk inside.

The inside of Katrina's house is not so nice. It smells
strongly of stale pot. The couch is filthy and saggy. There
isn't much in the way of furniture and the place is cold
on this mild November day. Indeed, it's colder inside than
outside. A brown shag rug, perhaps meant to be ironic,
just looks sad. Joe stands in the kitchen, rolling a joint and
drinking coffee. Now she remembers Joe. He played in a
band called Dogweed. It was a great, loud, fast, countrified
band, a three piece. They rocked. They were all short men

with long hair who played their instruments with love and abandon. There had been some buzz about them at the time, labels sniffing around. Now here stands Joe himself, his hair sheared off, and he looks defeated. Sad. Maybe even scared. All that pot has made deep lines in his face. He wasn't sexy anymore, not like Katrina.

THE WOMEN SETTLED INTO the living room, on opposite sides of the couch.

"Rufus, say hi to Katrina's friend, Sonia," says Katrina. Rufus scowls at Sonia and lifts up his mother's shirt, revealing a beautiful, pear shaped breast, and starts nursing. With his other hand, he fondles his mother's other breast. He growls quietly while he does this and looks menacingly straight at Sonia, as if she were some beast come to take away his mother.

"He's shy," says Katrina.

"Does he call you Katrina instead of Mommy? Because you said say hi to Katrina's friend, you know, instead of Mommy's," says Sonia.

"Oh, yes. Joe and I believe in children calling their parents by their first names. We're all people, individuals, you know? The objectification that "mommy" and "daddy," those words, produce, we feel is very damaging."

"Huh." A silence falls. *Fuck*, thought Sonia. Katrina was always weird, it was something that was so great about her. Weird fun. Eccentric. Outside the norm.

Katrina beams at Sonia. "You are so pregnant! My goodness. And you have kids? Where are they?"

"At home, in Brooklyn, with their father." Again, a thick silence. "I'm freaking out. I'm on a mission. A vacation. Something."

"I could never leave my Rufus." Katrina's face shows horror, but barely, it's a cute kind of horror, because her face is so damn dewy. God, what does she do to look that way?

"You know, Katrina, you look great. Your complexion, your skin . . ."

"I don't smoke, I eat no meat, I don't drink, I eat a vegetarian diet with tons of live foods. And I do colonics."

"You mean enemas?"

"Yes. There are so many toxins in the air and water and food around us. We all have fifteen pounds of poisonous metals in us that are killing us. Literally." Katrina strokes Rufus' head. He no longer glares at Sonia, to Sonia's great relief. Instead, his face is completely engulfed in the pillow of his mother's breast. "How old are your kids?"

"Four and two. Two boys. I don't really want to talk about it. I do miss them. I feel guilty about leaving them. But I freaked out. You see, this pregnancy was an accident."

"My fear of accidental pregnancy is so great that I just stopped having sex. I am not ready for another baby at all. Rufus still needs me so much. The thought of it! I feel for you, I do."

"When did you stop having sex with Joe?" Sonia whispers, even though Katrina wasn't whispering.

"About three years ago." Katrina says. "And don't worry about Joe hearing us. It's all in the open. We talk openly about everything."

"God, no sex must be hard on your marriage."

"Not really. He gets it somewhere else now and I don't mind. It's a relief, actually. Having kids changes everything. You know that."

"What about going on the pill?"

"No way! And poison my body?"

"Well, I don't know Katrina! Not having sex? You loved sex. You taught me how to love sex! I had never, and still have never, met anyone like you before. Someone who so unabashedly loved sex. You loved your body and men's bodies and music and drugs and wine . . . "

"That was a long time ago, Sonia." Katrina looks at her with serenity. Her mouth is set in a hard way, and for once, Sonia notices her age. "That all has to go at some point. One can't live like that forever. We were young! I'm not young anymore. Neither are you."

"But we're not dead yet, are we?"

"A part of us dies when our children are born, no? Our sexual self is never the same again. Our selfishness, our energy is zapped up. A lot of us dies with the birth of a child. As it should be. Trying to cling on to youth, or life as it was before children—sex, socializing—all of that seems so sad. Or hopeless. And so, instead I put all my hope in Rufus. He deserves it. He's going to have the childhood I never had."

"And what exactly is that, the childhood you never had?"

"I was the third child and my mother was so over-whelmed. And how can anyone pay attention to three children? And then my mother became so miserable and she started sleeping with the neighbor's son, a high-school boy. Then my parents got divorced."

Sonia knew all of this back in college. Hearing it again refreshes her memory of that time. Backstage, a delicious joint being passed around. A cooler full of Rolling Rock beer. Another friend, Lola, sitting on the lap of the lead singer of Zug Zug, a band of five beautiful, sweaty young men. Zug Zug meant fuck in caveman, according to them.

Rufus stops nursing and Katrina rubs his head and kisses him. He does not look like a happy kid. He looks fearful and miserable, anemic even. He glares at Sonia.

"I feel like your son hates me." There, she said it. Fuck Rufus's feelings. The way Katrina talks in front of him, she wasn't going to worry about saying the wrong thing.

"He doesn't like visitors so much. We mostly spend our time alone, here in the house, or walking around the prop-erty, enjoying nature. We have four acres, so we have a lot of privacy" Katrina says.

"Do you guys have friends? I mean, you must have friends."

"We have some of Joe's customers—he deals weed . . . but, eh, not really. Friends are overrated. Family is every- thing.

"I understand that to a degree, but you are a person, too. And you need to be a person in the . . . in the world! I guess that's how I feel. I'm out here, in the world right now. I'm letting the father of my boys take over."

"Men are not made for child care. In hunter-gatherer cultures, the women take care of the children, while the men take care of the hunting and the government. There's a lot we can learn from more primitive cultures. Listen, tomorrow is Sunday. Why don't you stay the night— although I really feel like sending you back to your boys right this second . . . "

"I'm not going back right now. Not tonight. I will go back eventually." Sonia feels small saying this. But it's true and sitting here talking to Katrina makes her realize it. She can't return yet. "We should go out, Katrina. You and me, at some local bar. Leave Rufus for a couple hours with his dad."

"I don't drink, Sonia."

"We could drink club sodas. You know, just get out. I mean I love your devotion, but how often do we get to see each other?"

Katrina looks at Sonia with all her dewy, washed-out- colon energy. She smiles a smile of real generosity. "I know you think I'm crazy, Sonia. I also know that almost everyone thinks we, people like me, are crazy. But we're sane in an insane world, you see? Thomas Szasz said that about schizophrenics. But really, it's us, women in touch with their bodies and the humans that come forth from them, that are truly the sane ones even if people think we're crazy. It's really hard to be in touch with our natural selves in such a busy, technology driven world. We have to make a real effort to tune out the bad noise, the corruption of the so-called civilized world."

"You wouldn't have all this information about hunter-gatherer worlds and Thomas Szasz to base your ideas on if it weren't for airplanes, universities, and Western education. That information is made available to you *because* of technology and Western civilization. Do you not see the irony of that?"

Katrina's face looks pinched. Rufus has walked away from her, and disappeared into a dark room behind them. "Irony isn't my thing, Sonia."

"Well, do you understand the contrived nature of your ideology?" Sonia feels like an idiot even as the words leave her mouth. *Ideology! Contrived nature!* Who does she think she is?

"I understand you need to see it that way. That's because you're afraid." The pinchedness leaves Katrina's face. She looked serene again. "Rufus has headed back to our bedroom because he wants to nap. I better go back there to nurse him to sleep. First, I'll show you our guest room. You'll stay the night, won't you?"

"I'd love to. Thanks." There's something about Katrina, something so magnetic, that has always drawn people to her, including Sonia. Even if her friend has changed, she still has that magic, of making you want to be around her. "One more thing. Do you still paint?"

Katrina looks straight at her. There's no wistfulness, no regret in her face. "No. Painting is for children. I only do the work of a grownup now."

Sonia pushes herself up from the couch. Following Katrina up the stairs and into a small room with peeling pink-flowered wallpaper, she is reminded of how she always felt following Katrina around. Big, ungainly. The ugly duckling behind the poised one. Now, here, pregnant and truly ungainly and on Katrina's turf again—it had always been Katrina's turf, the clubs, the parties—she feels the same again. Like an eager and stupid person, like the awkward one. A person who needs to be led.

AFTER NAPTIME, THERE'S DINNER. Katrina cooks, while Joe is in another room watching TV.

"How is it that you have a TV if you try to shut out the civilized world?" Sonia asks.

"Look—we have a TV. A stove. Indoor toilets. Although we like to camp. We camp a lot and then we really get back to nature."

Sonia helps by cutting carrots and cauliflower and washing collard greens.

"I'm going to be frank. This dinner is going to give my pregnant ass major gas."

"Gassiness comes from the sulfur and sulfur is *so*"— Katrina draws out the word—"good for you."

Sonia eats it all, the brown rice, collard greens, carrots, cauliflower and some strange, lumpy pudding for desert. She was starved and grateful for food. But afterward, she pays the price, shamefully and painfully spends the evening in her little room, trying to spare the others from her insane gas. She comes out to say goodnight to the three of them sitting around in the damp and cold TV room, watching some violent and graphic cop show that she would never in a million years let her children watch. It's dark. The screen glows and reflects off their three moonish faces as they turn to her and bid her goodnight.

BACK IN THE GUEST room, piles of sour blankets lay heaped atop her. Farting away in the dark, her stomach a rumbling mess, she begins to feel the baby move. Kicking, turning around in circles, a little monster inside of her. Sonia tries to breathe out of her mouth, feeling bewildered. This has happened twice now, to carry another life inside of her, and yet the weirdness, the surreal aspect of it, is still surreal. It does not feel natural. It feels ungodly. She feels terror. Pain. And then, the stink of her own self, which brings her back to the room, outside of her body, is a sort of relief. A distraction.

The door to her room slowly opens, and there, lit up momentarily in the hallway, stands Joe. He closes the door behind himself and comes and sits on the edge of the double mattress.

"Jesus, it stinks in here."

"Sorry."

Joe whistles as he lets out a heavy, blowing breath. "Good God."

"Sorry! I am in here to spare your family. I'd rather be watching TV out there, but I thought it would be cruel of me. I can't eat cauliflower when I'm pregnant. Or collard greens, for that matter." She pauses. "What you are doing here?"

"Oh, I think you know what I'm doing here."

Sonia tenses, the baby flips around and kicks her in the ribs, and then Sonia farts again. Her eyes begin adjusting again, after being blinded by the hallway light. She sees Joe's nose, thin and handsome, pointed toward her. The dark of his eye sockets. His small hands folded neatly in his lap.

"I don't know what you're doing in here. But if I were you, I wouldn't be in here. Unfortunately, I am me, and I can't leave myself in here."

"You should try meditating or levitating or whatever Katrina does to transport herself out of her body. She's really into meditating."

"Katrina must know you are in here. Joe. This is weird."

"She might know and she might not. She may think I'm out in the garage or still in the TV room. Or in my bedroom. Rufus and she went to bed in their bedroom."

"I see."

Joe delicately refolds his hands. "When Katrina was pregnant, she was insanely horny all the time."

"Yes, I was like that during my first pregnancy. And a little during my second pregnancy, although it was harder to have sex all the time because I had my first kid around."

"And this time? How are you feeling this time? I am here, by the way, to fuck you if you want. Even if the room stinks like a nasty factory town." He reaches a hand out to her and puts it on her ripe pregnant-lady breast. Just like that, no rubbing of the shoulder, no gentle pat. He just lifts his hand and puts it directly on her breast.

"I don't think so, Joe." Something stirs in Sonia. Is she thinking of getting laid? Then, another fart flies out of her.

"God. What is wrong with me?" says Joe, his hand still on her breast. "Why has it come to this? Don't get me wrong, I always thought you were attractive, in that skinny, bendable way. I don't like that you're four inches taller than me. But whatever. What should I do? Leave Katrina? I love her. I love my son."

"Shit. I don't know, Joe. Have you thought about counseling?"

"Counseling isn't going to change Katrina's belief system. Nothing will, unless she adopts a new belief system all on

her own. I have no power over her, Sonia. I never have and
it was a good thing in the past. A woman with a mind of her
own. You know? I didn't want to marry some doormat."

"Can you take your hand off my breast?"

He leans over and puts his face close to hers and grips
her breast more tightly. "Let me fuck you."

"No."

"Just touch my dick."

"Joe. I can't."

He pulls back up to sitting and takes his hand off her
breast. Then he removes a stub of a joint and lights it, the
match illuminating his handsome features for a moment.
"You know, you always thought you were too good for
me, didn't you? A college girl. You never gave my type
the time of day, really. We were just a stop on your way
upward, weren't we? High-school dropout rock kids. Your
little toys. Fuck. And now, you think you were right to be
so superior to us back then. I'm just some small-time pot
dealer, right? You were right about us, weren't you?"

"Listen, I don't give a shit how you make your money
and that's got nothing to do with why I won't fuck you.
Katrina's my friend. You're her husband."

"She's not your friend anymore and she would be grateful to you for fucking me. You just don't want to fuck me."

"Alright! Whatever. Give me a break. I'm pregnant and
I've run away from home and my ass is on fire! Don't tor-
ment me anymore."

"Fine." His lips seem to be quivering. "I understand. I do." He takes another drag of his joint and then puts it out on the tip of his tongue. It hisses. The smoke momentarily relieves Sonia of the sulfur smell coming out of her body. She breathes in deeply the smoky, herbaceous smell through her nose.

"I'm sorry, Joe. OK? I'm sorry," she says at his back, as he slips out the door.

IN THE MORNING, SONIA wakes late. She dreamt of her boys, of being with them in their apartment in Brooklyn. It was a quiet dream, a small, comforting dream. It took her awhile to remember where she was. Suddenly, she feels very pregnant. That's how it is, overnight, her stomach muscles had loosened and her belly now protrudes outward in a way it didn't the day before. Perhaps it was the workout her intestines went through, but her belly, in one night, has become very large. There is no mistaking it now. She gets up and her crotch feels heavy, newly so, and as she walks out to the bathroom she feels as if she is starting to waddle. The pregnancy waddle. There is a relief in this. A strange sort of relief that it's progressing and that it would, someday, be over.

"You're up! Here's some tea for you." Katrina shines her glowy face at Sonia and hands her a warm mug.

"Do you have any coffee?" Sonia feels like a dried-up, large beast, a hippo, next to Katrina.

"Coffee causes miscarriage and low birth-weight babies. Have this tea. It has no caffeine in it."

No caffeine? Sonia already has a headache. "I'll pass. But thank you. I'll get something on my way."

"I hope you're going back to your family," Katrina says, sipping her tea so delicately. Sonia stares at Katrina for a moment. She's never been more mesmerized by another woman. Never. And even if Katrina has changed, in so many ways she hasn't. She's just Katrina, later. As it should be, thinking of Stan, how he doesn't get that he's not going to get some break or understand that heroin is pathetic instead of cool. Change is good, even if sometimes it's alarming and over the top.

They hug goodbye in front of the car, awkwardly, Rufus on Katrina's hip between them. Joe is nowhere to be found.

"Katrina, thank you so much for having me. It was great to see you—you are so," Sonia feels vulnerable but open, "you are so beautiful."

"You're sweet, Sonia. Now go home and take care of your boys and yourself."

"Will do."

15

But she doesn't go home and take care of her boys. She heads west. The roads get wider and quieter and she gets deep into Pennsylvania. She stops for diner food when she can, which she prefers to the chains. Her comfort level isn't great so she stops regularly at the cleanest-looking motels she can find. She eschews the ones advertising day rates and manages to find decent chains—for the most part. And suddenly a week has gone by and the only conversations she's had are with waiters and hotel clerks and the one she has in her head with herself and the endless television shows she watches. And, not so surprisingly, she finds she's in South Bend, Indiana, her hometown.

She hasn't counted but figures she has almost six thousand left, so she splurges on a room at the Marriott Hotel downtown, a big glass building built by a famous architect.

She remembers what a big deal it was when it was built, how it brought pride to her parents, how their modest lives in South Bend were somewhat elevated by the structure. At that point, Sonia already had her eyes on the big cities of the Northeast and it embarrassed her, how her parents took pride in the Marriott. And yet now, as she checks in, and as it seems to be even nicer—hell, all of South Bend seems nicer—she understands their pride. And that pride in where one lives is important and Sonia's face flushes with the shame of the arrogance of her youth.

From her room at the Marriot, she calls home. She's called home a few times on the road, but only hung up. This time, she doesn't.

"Sonia?"

"How are they?"

"How do you think they are?"

"My guess is they're fine," she says weakly.

"They're not dead, if that's what you mean."

Silence.

"Don't hang up, Sonia. I promise I'm not gonna try to trace the call, find out where you are. I'm not trying to come and get you. I just want to talk to you."

"I want to hear more about the boys."

"They're OK. They're used to you not being here now. Sort of."

"Sort of?" Sonia suddenly gets a charley horse in her calf. She rubs it.

"Well, Mike is back in diapers full time."

"Big fucking deal. He's barely three."

"Listen. You asked why I say sort of, I'm telling you. But if you're not gonna listen, then why ask? He's regressed. And Tom's developed a stutter. Just so you know."

"Who says he wouldn't have stuttered anyway?" she asks—or screams, actually. She realizes with a shock that she just screamed the question at her husband, and that he is now screaming right back, telling her, *"Well, he wasn't stuttering when you fucking left!"*

She hears, Daddy?, in the background and Dick says to her, "hold on," and goes and puts the boys in front of the television—she can hear it being turned on, loud. She can visualize her boys, sitting on the couch, happy to have the TV on. Then he's back. "They're all right, they're going to be alright, but they'd be better off if you were here."

"I'm coming back."

"When?"

"Soon."

"How are you? How's the baby?" She hears his voice break. God.

"I'm fine. The baby's fine." Sonia puts her hand on her stomach as she says this and starts to rub at it. The baby shifts gently under her shirt, and she pulls it up and looks at her bare stomach. It's taut, big, but not huge. This one's different. Sonia isn't like a house, like she was with the boys. She's more like a shed. A sturdy, small outbuilding. "I'll be back. I'll call, too."

"Where are you?"

"I'm not gonna tell you that." Fuck. Fuck, fuck, fuck. Now she's starting to cry. "Can I talk to the boys? Please."

"I don't know. It might make things worse."

"Please. I just want to hear their voices."

"Then come home." His voice is thick, but the sadness is gone.

"Please."

"No. Not now. I can't handle it now. I need to keep it together for them. I can't watch them talk to you. Come home, Sonia. Come home for Christmas, at least."

"Fuck Christmas. I hate Christmas. Fucking Toys "R" Us-day is what it should be called. It's meaningless and you know it . . ."

"Yeah, but they don't. Think about someone else besides yourself for a change."

"That's exactly what I did, Dick, for five fucking years, and that's exactly what I'll have to do again, in a couple of months, and that's exactly why I'm not there now."

Silence. "I'll call soon." Her eyes burn. "I'll call soon. I'll come home soon." And she's about to hang up.

"Wait, Sonia, I have to tell you something."

"What?"

Dicks sighs heavily into the phone. "Social Services was here."

"What? What the fuck . . ."

"I didn't call them. One of your friends did. I think it was Clara. I mean, I guess I know it was her."

"Oh my God. Oh my God."

"Listen. Everything is OK. And I'm on your side. I'm very mad at you and can't make promises to you about anything, but I do want you back here with our sons. But you have to know the community is not on your side."

"'I haven't been gone that long . . . this is ridiculous."

"You didn't tell anyone where you were going, I had no idea where you were . . . if you were safe . . ."

"I'm hanging up. I can't talk about this."

"It's your fault, Sonia."

She hangs up, furious, maybe a little scared, but no, Sonia focuses on furious and then decides to walk it off. All that time in the car, sitting, driving. As she exits the hotel she's stunned with what she sees. It's actually quite nice, down-town South Bend. She walks at a fast pace, letting the new buildings and clean St. Joseph River blow her mind. The place was an absolute dump when she left and still was when her parents moved to Florida, to their retirement commu-nity. They'd be even prouder, she thinks. Change. Even if it's the only thing you can count on, Sonia thinks, it still can stun. And the lack of it—she thinks of Stan—can stun, too. She walks and walks. New stores, some Notre Dame build-ings that were not there. When she lived there, Notre Dame was confined to the campus and had no presence downtown.

And she was a full-on townie. Feathered hair, tight stonewashed jeans, strong Midwestern drawl, hanging out outside the Taco Bell smoking weed. Friends graduating from high school and moving into trailer parks or beat-up rentals in sketchy neighborhoods. South Bend, beyond Notre Dame, still had the stink of an abandoned industrial town, having lost Studebaker and other auto industry first to Detroit, then to Japan, she guesses. After all that time in the car, the walking is a great relief, but she turns back to go to the hotel, to get food. She delights herself in the thought of once again, someone bringing her food. She thinks, every pregnant woman should live in hotels, getting fed by others.

She sits at the bar, but decides against beer—she's not in Boston, she can see someone calling the police on her. This is a Red State. She doesn't really know what goes on in a place like this, she realizes, when it comes to pregnant women. It wasn't anything she thought about when she was a kid. She orders a buffalo chicken sandwich with blue cheese and a side of sweet potato fries and a Coke. She eats quickly, thinking about strangling Clara, thinking about putting her hands around her friend's neck and strangling her, even though Clara, the überjock, would kick her ass. But no, Sonia thinks, my rage and craziness would swell gigantically, sort of like when people lift cars to save their husband or kids and yeah, superhuman with rage, she'd wrestle Clara to the ground and strangle her until the last bit of life had been squeezed away.

"Sonia?" She turns and sees a waiter in uniform and after a moment, she recognizes her ex-boyfriend's brother, Larry. How funny, thinks Sonia, Boston and now South Bend, both places she'd hope to see people from her past and not only does it happen, but she doesn't even have to try. For a moment a feeling of discomfort climbs up her back—the smallness of those worlds is one of the reasons she left them both in the first place.

"Larry Rogers, good to see you."

She puts out her hand. They shake.

"What are you doing in South Bend? Gosh, I wish Bruce were here, he'd love to see you." He's looking at her stomach. Pregnancy. The elephant in the room. It must not be ignored. How can it be? When pregnant, all other aspects of being recede. She could have a huge purple growth sticking out of the middle of her forehead but her pregnancy would still take precedence.

Sonia pats her stomach, "Yeah, I'm with child. I'd love to see Bruce, too. But he's not here." Bruce, her very first. Nice guy. Acid washed jeans matching hers, middle part, that slow Midwestern drawl, his gorgeous, young muscular body. Sonia wonders if he's bald and fat now. Might ask to see a recent picture.

"No, no. He moved to Chicago years ago." Larry smiles, puts his tray on his hip. Sonia realizes now that he was probably in the closet when they were teenagers. And that now, hopefully, he isn't.

"That's too bad. I mean, that I can't see him. Nothing wrong with moving to Chicago. You don't happen to have a recent picture of him?"

"Not on me. But you could come by my place depending on how long you're in town. I have some pictures of him and his family. You live in New York, right? This isn't your first baby, is it?"

Sonia had heard that Bruce was married with kids, and news about her must have leaked back, as well. "Yes, I live in Brooklyn actually and I have two sons."

"Wow, that's crazy. New York City. I can't even imagine."

"Imagine hordes of people and garbage on the street and bumping shoulders and getting yelled at for no reason and lots and lots of cement. There are good restaurants," Sonia says, her mind back on food for a moment. "It's amazing what a person can get used to. I've lived there a long time. It was exciting at first. Now the novelty has worn off."

"I imagine it's very glamorous."

"That's just television, Larry," although Sonia is thinking it would be much more fun to be gay in New York than South Bend.

"But what are you doing here?" he asks again.

Sonia sighed. "I'm just visiting. I was driving out west and thought I'd stop here."

She knows she's sounding vague. Larry looks at her with

a sort of perplexed frown, his very short hair neatly gelled back, and he switches the tray to his other side.

"I'd better get back to work. But I get off at ten. You should come out with me. I'm going over to Larissa's. She's still living in the mobile park, the nice one, near Mishawaka."

Sonia knew the mobile park. It *was* a nice one. She remembered when Larissa moved into it and how proud, rightly so, she was to have her own place when everyone, at 18, was still living, either with their parents, or like Sonia, largely off of their parents at college. It was nice for a trailer park, as Sonia remembered it, with mowed grass, trees, potted flowers. She's exhausted. But how can she say no? She hasn't been here for ages. And she can sleep all day tomorrow if she wants to. She can do whatever she wants. "Sure, come get me in room 412. I'd love to see Larissa."

A FEW HOURS LATER they're driving in Larry's very dirty, beat-up Honda. The ashtray is overflowing and there are magazines, empty cigarette packs and crumpled beer cans on the floor and what looks like wads of gum stuck all over the place. Sonia's not the neatest person and it often heartens her that someone's even grosser than herself. Especially since at the Marriott, he looked so dapper. And yet, she has to ask, "What are those?" She points to the hardened, raised things all over the car, "They look like chewed gum."

"They are," Larry says, waving a cigarette in the air and Sonia notices everything about Larry is different than at the Marriott. She notices pit stains in his white shirt, which he has untucked and unbuttoned, and a little hard beer belly is breaking through the top of his now unbelted pants. "Do you want a piece of gum? I keep tons in the glove compartment," he says, waving his cigarette in the direction of the glove compartment.

"No, thanks."

"Hey, can you pass me a beer? There's a cooler on the backseat there. Will you grab me one?"

"Sure," Sonia says, unbuckling herself nervously as Larry drives fast. Reaching around to the cooler and getting the lid open proves enormously difficult and when she achieves the goal, a wet can of Coors in her hand, she feels as if she just did enough prenatal yoga to last the rest of her pregnancy.

"Oh man, thanks."

He chugs it, the cigarette now smoldering in the mound of dead ones. "Fucking work, man. It's so good to be off."

"I waited on tables, I know how hard it is."

"Would you like a beer?"

"Maybe later." Sonia thinks she may be wrong about conservative Midwestern ideology. Although, this was her old friend and she always hung out with the rebellious types. The stoners, the heavy metal freaks, the troubled ones. In fact, now that she's sitting next to him, she remembers that Larry spent a few months in a mental institution when he was fifteen and she remembers thinking that he should have been in rehab instead. But his parents had been mean people.

"I guess you're not supposed to drink when you're pregnant. But Larissa says that's bullshit. When she was pregnant she did whatever she wanted to do. Her boys came out fine."

"I definitely think people can get overly paranoid, but fetal alcohol syndrome and heroin-addicted babies do happen." Sonia can't believe she almost sounds like *she's* taking the hard line. Then again, she's talking to a clueless, childless man. "Then again my first pregnancy was an accident so I was drinking quite a lot at the time and I quit as soon as I found out but I did all this research, made calls to clinics and talked to people. I was a really nervous pregnant woman."

"Oh yeah?" Larry chugged his beer. "I bet the third time you're less nervous."

"Yeah, I'm less nervous although this one is an accident too and even though I'm less nervous I'm more . . . crazy or something," Sonia says. "But anyway, one woman I talked to said—because I was weirdly worried about birth defects—she said, even if you do heroin the whole time, your baby will be born addicted to heroin, but most likely perfectly formed and fine otherwise. I thought that was the weirdest thing. And it comforted me. Not that I was planning on doing heroin."

"You don't get a lot of heroin around here," says Larry. "Meth, yes. I try to steer clear of meth heads. They get ugly really quickly."

They pull into the trailer park that has a paved entrance and a painted, lit-up sign, welcoming them to Sunshine Estate Trailer Park. As they wind around to Larissa's place, Sonia notices that Sunshine Estate Trailer Park had lost some of its luster. Either that or Sonia, after all this time away and now years of being ensconced in a striving upper-middle-class New York life, sees things differently. That maybe, she's sort of a snob. She shakes this feeling off. As much as she always wanted success, wanted *more* than what South Bend could offer her at the time, she'd always eschewed snobbery. It was possible, she knew it. It was a choice. And when Larissa first moved in to Sunshine Estate Trailer Park, it was brand new. And now it isn't. And things like trailer parks tended not to age well. It's not like you could treat your trailer exactly like a brownstone in Brooklyn and lovingly restore it. One could make repairs, for sure, but trailers were not built to last. In fact, they seem built to be joyfully temporary. And then people spend their entire lives in them anyway.

But Larissa's place isn't all exposed Tyvek and rusty car parts, like a few they pass on the way. The siding is intact, and there are a scattering of plastic kids' toys in the yard— not too different from Sonia's apartment.

"You would not believe who I have with me," Larry says, as Larissa opens the door.

And there they are, childhood best friends, wide-eyed and hugging, sort of a sideways hug due to Sonia's belly. Larissa's hair is still dyed and feathered with a curling iron, her eyeliner black and thick. She wears a skin tight pink T-shirt that says, "I'm A Bitch," and reveals bulging bra lines. She has put on at least fifty pounds.

"Oh my God, Sonia, what the hell?"

"I know, I know. I'm just as surprised to be here as you are to see me."

"Come in, come in. Holy crap. I thought I'd never see you again what with your fancy life in New York City and all."

"Sorry I've been out of touch. But so have you, Larissa," Sonia says, already sensing that underlying hostility Larissa was so good at letting loose. Their friendship had been an interesting one, basically one where Larissa mocked Sonia, and Sonia followed her around like a whipped puppy anyway because she admired Larissa so much and they did have fun together. And she was smart, smart in, what had felt at the time, the land of idiots. Bruce and Larry, too, felt like ships of intelligence in a sea of morons. They all had spent so much time together, drinking cheap beer, dreaming big dreams.

"True, true, it takes two to tango," Larissa says.

Larry bursts past them, six-pack in hand. "Well, let's

celebrate! This is awesome. Sonia here, I'm off work, life is good!" He sits down at a built-in kitchen table with a bench and a couple of chairs that Sonia remembers sitting at years and years ago. She plops down in the chair next to him and looks around. Two small boys, maybe three and five, sit on the far side of the trailer on a dark green plaid couch, watching a Disney movie on an enormous TV, a TV that takes up so much room the children's feet almost touch it from where they sit on the couch. Sonia wonders if they have to turn their heads from side to side while watching.

"Your sons?"

"Yup. My boys. Eric Junior and Bobby."

"I have two boys." Sonia says and tries immediately to get their faces out of her head. "Hey, Larry, can you pass me a beer?" She pulls the tab on the can and it makes that wonderful cracking noise as it exposes its imperfect circle of access and beery foam fizzles over.

"Man, I feel like we should play quarters or something!" Larry says. There had been many nights of epic games of bouncing quarters into glasses. "Hey, Larissa, get your bong out. Holy crap, Sonia, it's the same bong from high school! How classic is that?"

"That's pretty classic," Sonia says, knowing there is no way she could do a bong hit if her life depended on it. A hit off a joint, sure. But she quit bong-hitting in college or shortly thereafter. In fact she can't remember her last bong hit. "But let's roll a joint instead. I'm sort of not up for bong hits." Sonia looks toward the little boys. They're wearing matching pajamas with cars all over them. They look clean.

Larissa sits across from Sonia, drinking a beer. It seems not to be her first of the evening. "I had my boys with Eric Wilder, you remember him?"

"Sure," Sonia says. She had a huge crush on him, with his chipped tooth and penchant for carrying a sawed-off baseball bat around in his car.

"We never married. But we were together for five years. He's dead, you know."

"What?"

"He got really coked up at a party and they played Russian Roulette and he shot himself in the head."

"Oh my God, I'm so sorry Larissa."

"Thanks. It's been a few years, so I'm, well, not over it but I've learned to accept it."

The two women stare at each other. At last, Larissa says, "Russian Roulette is a stupid game."

And Sonia finds herself nodding almost dreamily in agreement, *yes, yes it is*, while Larry sits there, working on a beautiful joint.

Larissa sighs. "He was sort of a shitty boyfriend. I just had a weakness for him. Are you married?"

"Yeah, I'm married." Sonia stops and looks away. The kitchen area is tidy and reminds Sonia of a dollhouse. "He's a good guy. But it can be hard anyway."

"No shit," says Larry. "That's why everyone gets divorced."
Sonia looks from Larry to Larissa. "Are you guys . . ."

"Hell no!" Larry says, "I'm gay as can be!"

"We're just friends. We're the only ones left from the
old crowd. Dan is in Chicago. Eric is dead. You're in New
York," says Larissa, crushing the beer can into the table
with impressive force and accuracy, making it into a little
accordion beer can. She stands and gets another. "Do you
want one?"

"Not yet, thanks," says Sonia. "So Larry, you're 'out.'
That's great, right?"

"I'm out here tonight with you guys but it depends
where I am, how out I can be," he says. "I've gotten my ass
beat more than once. In fact, I've gotten my ass beat twice
very badly, once by a bunch of Notre Dame jocks and once
by a bunch of redneck bikers."

"That sucks," Sonia says.

"I learned my lesson. I'm more careful now." Larry lit
the joint. "So are you some famous painter in New York? I
think the last time I saw you that was your plan."

"Yeah," says Larissa, folding her hands over her fat breasts,
"You were going to be famous, an *important artist*. I think
you were living in Boston at the time and you were dressing
like a slut and spouting feminist theory and art talk."

"I was twenty. Don't even pretend you weren't an idiot
when you were twenty, Larissa." Sonia stands and gets
another beer. "And what's wrong with being ambitious?

What were you doing back then, cocktail waitressing at that strip club? I forgive all of our twenty-year-old selves and I'm OK with having had some ambitions. I mean, I know I was an idiot, but that's just life."

"I made tons of money at that job. I bought this trailer with that money." Larissa hits the joint and passes it to Sonia. Sonia holds it lovingly between her thumb and forefinger. She smells it, the sweet smell of weed. It's been ages since she's smelled it. She takes a tiny drag, holds it in as long as she can, blows out a thin stream of smoke.

"That was the most pussy hit I've even seen!" Larry says, laughing.

"I don't really smoke that much anymore. And I am pregnant."

"I bet weed is good for the baby. I bet it makes them little stoner geniuses, little Bob Marleys." Larissa says, hitting it again.

Sonia feels a head rush, feels the beer in her smooshed bladder. "Where's the bathroom?"

Larissa points to a door and Sonia, slightly off kilter, walks over to it. It's like an airplane bathroom, but with a shower and miniature tub. It has some nice touches. A flowered bath mat, clean towels. She sits and pees and then she notices the wall in front of her. It's covered with little circles of gum, like in Larry's car, but here she can see discernible patterns. Smiley faces, stick figures, something that looks like a, a—dog? Now, Sonia's a little high, but really just a little high and she's barely had two beers but she questions her judgment nonetheless. She stares. She tries to understand. Some of the gum is in different colors. Finally, she gets up.

"Hey, is that, like, gum design in there?" She asks and everyone starts that slow, stoner laugh that warms Sonia. All the tension of their disparate lives goes away and she's just back in South Bend, smoking weed with her buddies.

"Yeah," Larry says as his giggles subside and then he actually pops some gum in his mouth. "Do you want a piece?"

"Sure," says Sonia, putting a red stick of cinnamon gum in her mouth. "What the fuck is up with gum design?"

"It's just something I started doing. Right, Larissa?"

"Yeah." Larissa seems half asleep at this point. But Sonia feels energy, a tingling on her skin. Larry starts rolling another joint. Sonia looks over at the boys. They're asleep, cuddled adorably against each other, the television still going strong. For some reason it warms Sonia. She's just perfectly buzzed and she thinks of her sons, safe at home, sleeping in their beds.

"I just had the most amazing idea," Sonia says. "This gum design, Larry."

"What about it." Larry's eyes are red.

Sonia chews, the warm cinnamon coating her dry mouth and she sips her beer. Larry passes the joint to her and she takes another drag, a bigger one, and holds it in again, as long as she can. As she exhales, the world seems suddenly clear and right. "I think you could be famous. I mean, I know the art world in New York a little bit and I think that gum design, gum *art*, could make a huge splash. I've never seen anything like it. It's like part folk art, part naïve art, part found object art . . ."

"You're going to steal my idea," Larry says. "I can feel it."

"No way, Larry, I'm just a painter. I might not even be a painter anymore. Maybe the weed is making you paranoid. Really, I could be your agent or get you a manager or a gallery or something." Sonia stands. Her back was hurting but also she just needs to stand. Larissa appears asleep.

"Really, Sonia, you'd do that for me?"

Larissa snored, her head bobbed up. "Guys, I gotta go to bed. I have to work tomorrow. Are you still going to be here, Sonia?"

"I don't know." Sonia says. "But Larry, I think I've figured it all out. At first I thought the gum was gross, just disgusting, all over your car. But now, I think I've discovered you, and you are the future of art." He passes the joint to her. Three hits? She feels so perfect. "No, no I'm perfect. This is all perfect. I sort of left my family and I— I really don't want to be pregnant. I thought I wanted to paint and not have more babies and— I'm really high right now. Anyway, but now that I've discovered *you, you Larry*—I feel OK."

Sonia sits down. Larry, red-eyed, is rapt. Sonia goes on. "But here's the deal. I think I missed my chance when I was painting my friends as Hindu gods. I'd use these pictures of Krishna and Shiva and so on and then I'd paint the faces of my friends, you know, in the place of Krishna's face. And someone told me, you have to paint the faces of *famous* people, not your friends." Sonia has never known something to be so true as what she is saying right now. She sits here, in Larissa's trailer, and she leans on the table and puts her hands on Larry's face. "And he was right! My friend. And I didn't listen to him. And now I know. And you need to make your gum design in the shape of *famous people*. Not dogs or smiley faces. But, like, Madonna! Robert De Niro. Right? Do you get it?"

Larry gently removes Sonia's hands. "Wow. You're a genius. That is the perfect idea."

Larissa stands, wavering. "Sonia! I'm asleep. You guys gotta go. I'll see you tomorrow. Sonia, let's not be mean to each other."

"You were always mean to me."

"That's because you always thought you were better than me, better than everyone else."

Sonia is silent. This is true. "Larissa, I think I discovered the future of art on your bathroom wall. And Larry, it's all Larry."

"That's great. Go home. I'll see you tomorrow."

"I'm staying at the Marriott. That's how I ran into Larry."

Larissa is expertly moving them out the door.

"Tomorrow. After work. We'll see you again."

16

Sonia wakes up, confused as she often has been, and it takes a moment to remember where she is. She's in a bed at the Marriott Hotel, in South Bend, Indiana. She grew up in South Bend. The sheets are really nice. Nicer than the various other hotels she's been staying in, nicer than the sheets at the Holiday Inn Express in Eastern Ohio. Her room is fabulously dark, even though she looks at the clock and it says 11:30 A.M. She remembers pulling the shades closed last night and they are heavy, wonderful shades. She's in a cave of sleep, but slowly coming out of it. She had no dreams, but now thoughts of Dick and her boys flit through her head and she represses the urge to call them. She stands to go pee.

Last night, she thinks, peeing. That weed was something else. She'll have to call Larry if she doesn't see him at the hotel. She remembers the gum, the ecstatic vision

of the future of art. Wow she was high. And from so little—what did she have, two hits? Gum art! How fucking
gross. And how did she think he would be able to make
more than smiley faces—well, she guesses he could—but
famous people? Maybe she should smoke weed more
often, though. Maybe it would help her painting. If she
ever paints again.

After a room service breakfast of eggs, beef hash and
toast, and a hot shower with excellent water pressure, Sonia
drives to her old house, the house she and Nicky grew up
in, the house her parents had lived in for thirty years. She
pulls up right in front and parks. It's exactly the same.
Beige brick on the bottom half, white siding on the top. A
slate roof—that might be new. Four windows in the front.
Houses like this, generic, sensible, modest—they always
remind Sonia of faces.

She really had no complaints about her childhood—
what was the point? At a certain point—preferably before
thirty—people should move on to take responsibility for
their lives. And she had. Nicky had been different. She
nursed resentments, remembering details of neglect or
hurt that Sonia questioned and still questions if they were
even true. That's what bad therapy will do to you, turn you
into a perpetually wounded child. Sonia gets out of the car,
walks to the door and knocks.

A woman in her sixties answers the door, gray hair,
brown eyes, trim, wearing a blue oxford shirt.

Sonia tells the woman her name. "I grew up here . . ." she says.

Sonia peeks in over the woman's head. The entranceway is painted bright yellow and there's a sign with a teddy bear stuck to it that says, "Welcome To Our Home." This is something that would have made her mother cringe. In its place had hung one of the many of her mother's etchings. Her mother, the amateur artist and content to be that, or seemingly so. Sonia had always wanted more than that.

"Oh yes, we bought the house from your parents when they retired to Florida."

"I happen to be in town and was wondering if I could look around."

"Of course. Come in," the woman says, "My name is Alison Bower."

They shake hands and Sonia says, "Nice to meet you." The kitchen, off to the left, is entirely different, which isn't a bad thing. It's all tasteful, large tile floors with a subdued wooden table. Still, something aches in Sonia, the memory of her mother standing at the counter, singing to herself, bright-green leaf wallpaper glaring all around. The dented linoleum floors, dented from Sonia constantly leaning back on her chair. Those dents, which drove her mother crazy, they come back to Sonia now and she thinks, each one was a moment in life, a moment in exuberant childhood.

"The house we grow up in is always very significant.

Your whole childhood took place here," Alison says, and makes a sweeping motion with her hands.

Sonia is looking around and her heart aches. Everything disappears. Not just trailers. Lives. Kitchens. Her child-hood bedroom, where it all started, her life. Alison seems to register this.

"Of course, we renovated when we moved in."

"Of course," says Sonia. "I understand."

"Would you like a cup of tea or something?"

"I'd love a glass of water." Sonia says.

"Please have a seat. You must be due very soon!"

"Yes." Sonia sits in the familiar but unfamiliar kitchen. It seems smaller than she remembers. The house seems smaller, but she knows it's just that most of her memories took place when she was a child and she was small. Like her boys are. Making memories, every day seems like a lifetime, and now those lifetime-long days are being made without her.

"I'm going to go up to my old bedroom if that's OK."

"Sure thing. Take your time. I don't know what room was yours—one is a guest bedroom now and the other an office."

"It's all fine. I'm just never here so I thought I'd take advantage and pay a visit."

"Like I said, take your time."

Sonia walks up the hardwood stairs that were once car-peted in beige. The handrail is the same wooden, smooth handrail. She holds on to it. It got her in trouble. She constantly slid down handrails, well into her teens when it seemed childish and inappropriate.

She goes into her room and shuts the door. The office. The walls are quite bare with the exception of a framed Matisse print, a still life, flowers. There's a bulletin board as well, but Sonia, feeling somewhat well-mannered, doesn't scrutinize it. Otherwise there's a large, green armchair, a filing cabinet and a beautiful midcentury desk. She sits in a chair in front of the desk and closes her eyes. When she was little, it was all green carpeting and a twin bed and stuffed animals. Then it morphed into her den of hedonism—she had a queen mattress on the floor—for some reason that felt sexy to her—and her bedspread was an Indian print. Nicky's room was more conservative, blue rugs and a matching blue bedspread with a flower print on a twin bed. Nicky, who lives in Boulder now. She has a son that Sonia met once when Nicky came to New York for a wedding—the boy was an infant then. He must be seven or so now. She hasn't seen Nicky in so long. They weren't close. It was the cliché of two children growing up in the same house, but in different families. Very Psychology 101, but very true. Then again, sometimes Sonia thinks people choose to see their families differently, and it's more that choice than any "different family" shit. Then there was just plain different interests, different personalities. Nicky wanted to go to college out West and climb mountains and ride horses. Sonia wanted to go to the East and live in a big sophisticated city and make art and talk pretentiously about art. But they were sisters. They did grow up together. And there's something about the sibling relationship that is even more significant than the parental relationship. One's parents had a full life beforehand. You come into their lives when they are adults. But siblings know each other from birth, witness the constant formation of character through childhood, through a child's eyes, too.

Sonia gets up and knows where she's going. She's not going to call Larry or Larissa. She gets to the stairs and tries to get up on the bannister to slide down it, but her pregnant self won't allow it. She walks down, carefully, and heads straight out the door to her car and heads to the highway. It isn't until she's a half an hour on the highway that she realizes she forgot to thank Alison, even forgot to say goodbye.

17

She takes her time, like she took her time getting to Indiana. The days bleed into each other and the driving is more and more uncomfortable, so she spends a lot of time watching movies in hotels. She spends Christmas in a Ramada Inn. She spends New Year's in a Motel 6. Both days she feels sorry for the people who work at the desk. She's always felt sorry for people who have to work menial jobs on holidays. You're supposed to be with your family. And then when her thoughts go there, she doesn't feel sorry for herself, but she feels ashamed. Then she watches more TV, the great thought killer.

On her final stretch to Boulder, she develops an awful case of hemorrhoids. The worst. Truck driver hemorrhoids. So what does she do? She does what any self-respecting truck driver would do. She gets herself a donut to sit on.

Sonia sits happily on her donut and starts the car. She sits still for a minute, the car humming, and feels her ass cheeks spread open because of the donut hole. This is the point of the donut, to free all pressure from her asshole. Does she feel relief? She sits there for a bit, in the parking lot of the Walmart in western Illinois. To figure out if the donut is really helping her. Her ass is smeared with Preparation H—which she did in the bathroom at Walmart—and now she has her donut. It seems to help, but it puts pressure on her lower back, which already ached a bit. She scoots around, finds a way of perching on her donut and resting her lower back against the seat that seems to feel the best. And then she backs out.

Four hours later, and it's dark. She's not ready to stop at a motel yet. Her ass feels so great! She could drive forever! Tonight, she'll drive late into the night, or so she thinks. She will drive, drive, drive! She is sick of all her tapes and CDs, or rather, she is taking a break from them before she gets completely sick of them, and she's listening to the radio, listening to a classical station. Sonia doesn't listen to tons of classical music, but she does listen to a bit of it. She listened to more of it in high school, with her dad, before she moved out, and rock 'n' roll took over her life. And yet, she knows this music! How exciting! It is Ravel, the piano concertos. Her father played them on his enormous stereo. When she was a little girl, she danced around the living room, a terribly awkward ballerina, flapping her arms to the music. But the music was inspiring, soaring at times, perhaps even emotionally manipulative. But that is what she likes about it, perhaps what she likes most about all music. It can make you feel what it wants you to feel. It can take control. She turns it up and her heart clenches. Her boys. No, no she can't think of them. Willing herself to think of something else, she thinks of her donut. Ah, the power of the mind. The mind can switch around, can move, can unstick itself. Her shiny, plastic, dark blue donut that is cradling the fat of her ass. She starts moving her ass around, and her lower back is enjoying it, too. She's massaging her lower back against the back of the car seat, and her butt cheeks on the sturdy but cushiony curves of her donut. Now, in her mental vision, comes the sight of what is floating free in the whole of the donut. Her oversized, red, slightly angry pussy. The baby is pushing down on all of her organs and her vagina gets so much blood trapped down there. She remembers the thought she had during her first pregnancy—monkeys with their red swollen genitalia have nothing on me. And so it was, and so it is again.

Sonia scoots her ass around so she's gripping the sides of the donut with her ass cheeks. She manages to move the donut with the grip of her butt, so that she now perches on the side of it, rather than sitting on it as she's meant to sit on it. No more floating in the hole. No more parts of her being suspended in free air. No, now she feels the lips of her crotch embracing the plastic of the donut. She swerves a bit during this maneuvering and looks in the rearview mirror. Her breath is coming a bit more quickly now. She's nervous. No one behind her, no one immediately behind her. There are some lights far back, far, far back, as this Midwestern highway is so straight and flat she can see for what seems like forever.

She begins grinding, back and forth, back and forth. God. It's been too long since she last masturbated. During her first pregnancy, she masturbated every day. Like a guy. Like a fifteen-year-old boy. Hell, she was in her late twenties and still thought fucking and coming were the most important things in life. My, how things have changed. During her second pregnancy, she had little time to herself, what with her son running around. But when he napped in the afternoon, she sometimes got to masturbate. Sometimes, she read a magazine, or returned phone calls. But sometimes, she took a "nap"—which meant, jacked off. But this pregnancy, she could count how many times she'd done it, taken care of herself.

It's not easy to lift her body—she's getting big and unmanageable—but she does it, lifts herself out of the seat, grunting to do so, and she takes one hand off the wheel and pulls her skirt up and her sticky panties down. The car is swerving, but she's in control, she is, and she slows down, too. Indeed, she stops pressing the accelerator at all. She gets her panties to her midthighs and then falls back down on the donut. Now, from a more relaxed sitting position, she pulls her panties down to her ankles. First one side, then the other, until the panties drop down to her ankles, and she can kick them off, just by lifting a foot. No more panties! It's just her wet, needy pussy and the cool, slick plastic of the donut. Back and forth, back and forth. God! Ravel is getting excited, too. Swirling around, quickly, wrenchingly. It's painful music, but beautiful, beautiful. She feels tears come to her eyes—these concertos always made her cry, she remembers—but she can't ever remember crying while masturbating. This is a new one. She also is pretty sure she's never masturbated in a car, or at least not while trying to drive it. She's given blow jobs in cars, been fingered and fucked in cars, once had her pussy eaten out in a car (that was Philbert Rush), but she's never masturbated in a car, especially not while driving. Back and forth, around and around. Her ass tenses. Is she going to make it? Well, yes. Too soon? Perhaps there is no too soon in a car, on a highway. Perhaps quick is the point. She looks down at her body—it is the *Venus de Milo*. Round, wet, a bit smelly. She reaches down into her T-shirt to grab a breast and manages without too much trouble. Her breast is wet. God. With sweat, with that humid nipple sweat that happens when she's in an excited state. God help her. She pinches her nipple, hard. A white drop appears on the edge of her nipple and then drips down. Soon, she'll have milk. Her breasts when she is nursing are the most erotic thing to her. For a moment, she can't see. This scares her. Should she pull over to finish herself off? She can't look into the mirror, it would ruin it. She's so close. She can do it. I think I can, I think I can, I think I can, she says to herself, as she grinds against the donut.

She puts her hand on her other breast and squeezes it, massages it, pinches that nipple. She loves loves loves her pregnant tits. Loves them. She thinks of the Almodovar movie, where one of his female characters says of women: "We're all assholes. And a bit lesbo." Anyone who's ever masturbated is a bit homosexual, no? But just a bit. Because mostly, while she enjoys touching her body, she has to think of men fucking her to get to the end. She usually closes her eyes tight and thinks of men in and on and around her pussy.

But she can't close her eyes, unless she were to pull over, which it looks like she might have to do. Grinding, grinding, lifting her ass a bit higher so her pussy is barely grazing the donut, teasing it, and then slamming it down and grinding it hard. Oh, God! It's a car. A red light glows on top of it. Oh shit, it's a police car behind her! Maybe he's driving past? To get some speeding villain? She's not driving fast at all! Please Mister Policeman, don't pull me over. His lights glare at her and she looks at him through the side view mirror. She's right there . . . she's so close. She slaps her breasts. Bad, bad, bad. She is a very bad lady. She pinches hard. Ah, ah, not yet. He flashes his lights at her. Fuck, fuck, he'll see her pussy! He'll know! He'll smell her in the car! He'll . . . fuck her. Come and fuck her. Through the loudspeaker comes the "pull over your car." And she puts both hands on the wheel and pulls over, grinding on her donut all the more quickly. She's sweating now, her face is all red, her hair damp. She stops the car, she knows she has a minute or two, before the cop comes out of the car, she's been pulled over before, she knows the drill, he's doing a check on her license plate number, or at least writing it down, it's exciting, shaming, shameful and exciting, and now that she's pulled over, she has both hands free and she puts a finger inside of herself and with the other hands rubs herself and yes, yes! He's coming out of the car to get her! Ravel has reached his crescendo, her heart is flying with the music and, and yes! He's walking this way, and maybe he's young, and mean, and strong and yes, yes!

Sonia slumps forward and her hands come out of her dress. She wipes them on her thigh. She's shaking, red-faced, her hair glued to her forehead in dark, wet clumps. Her lips are dry from the hot breath coming out of her mouth. There is a cop shining a light at her. She rolls down her window. "Can I see your license and registration, ma'am?"

18

The room is dark, but it must be morning. Only the thinnest sliver of light can be seen through the motel's shades. Blackout shades, and Sonia is grateful. It feels as if she has slept late. After a humiliating show of walking a straight line, which wasn't easy, (without underwear, and her legs were jelly from her orgasm and when she's pregnant her balance is off) and a breathalyzer test, the trooper finally understood that she was just tired and distracted. One good thing that pregnancy does is occasionally evoke sympathy. It took a while in this case, took a while for the cop to trust her. In the beginning, he had flashed a light into her car and she wondered if he saw her sticky panties. He most certainly saw the donut. Anyway, he escorted her to a nearby motel and that was the end of that.

The next morning, she sends Dick a postcard from the

motel, one that came in the stationery of the motel, a sad photograph of the motel itself, low lying and generically white, door after door leading all to the same rooms. She writes, "I'm OK, just so you know." She leaves it at the front desk when she checks out for the clerk to mail. And then she gets in her car and keeps driving.

In Boulder, she uses her credit card and is happy it works. Dick didn't cancel it. She splurges even more than usual and stays at the St. Julien Hotel in downtown Boulder. It's positively elegant, posh, full of fancy nuts in the minibar and plush robes and a fluffy bed with no less than six absurdly large pillows.

She calls Nicky's house and her husband Steve answers the phone.

"Wow, Sonia, what a surprise." Steve had always been friendly, ignoring the obvious lack of closeness between Nicky and Sonia. Sonia likes this about him, his laid-back character, his ability to tune out tension and pretty much anything else that's irritating.

"Yes, I've been surprising a lot of people lately."

"Nicky's out right now, but I'm sure she'll be excited to know you're in town."

Sonia's not so sure about this. She expects her sister might be perplexed, even annoyed. At best, she'll be indifferent. She has no memory of Nicky being excited to see her. Probably at her birth, she wasn't excited to see her, and things continued from there.

"Well, I'd love to come over and see you guys. Unless it's a bad time."

"No, no. It's fine."

"I'm staying at a hotel so I won't really impose."

"Don't worry about it. Come by. Nicky should be home soon."

Sonia drives out to the new house Nicky and Steve moved into a few years ago. It's just outside of Boulder, a twenty-minute drive from Sonia's hotel where the land begins its endless dry, beige flatness. As beautiful as the mountains around Boulder are, the flat barren foreverness of the rest of the landscape strikes Sonia as ugly. She arrives at the house, a nice-sized house in a development that abuts a nature preserve, with mountains sprouting in the distance. Nicky and Steve are both there, as is their boy, Nathan, who appears to be seven or eight. They look alike to a creepy degree. Now, Sonia is very aware that married couples often begin to look alike, act alike, hell, even their dogs start to look like them. The power of living together for years? Who knows. But Nicky and Steve are special. They are both the same height, around five feet nine; they both have ropey muscular builds; they both have almond-shaped blue eyes; blond hair down to their shoulders; and petite mouths in their oval, sun-worn faces. And they dress the same—athletic gear, for the most part, outdoorsy athletic gear. Their son also looks just like them, which Sonia thinks lucky. The lack of genetic cross-breeding could easily have produced a mutant child with serious health problems. *Good lord*, she thinks as she walks up to the door where they all stand waiting to greet her, they could be identical twins if they only had the same genitalia.

Hugs are exchanged, Sonia's belly getting in the way. Cheek kisses are mistimed—Sonia ends up banging her nose into her sister's ear.

"Sonia, you didn't tell me you were pregnant."

"I'm pregnant."

"Congratulations," says Steve.

"It was an accident. But thank you," Sonia says as they enter the house.

"Accidents can be a blessing. Your first was an accident and look how great that was," Nicky says. "We're just about to have lunch. Come join us."

"I'll sit with you guys but I had an enormous breakfast delivered to my room not long ago," says Sonia, who can always eat more, but she examines the spread in front of her and decides against it. "May I ask what all this is?"

"This is quinoa bread with a bean spread. That's a dandelion salad and this here is my homemade venison sausage," Steve says. "We try to eat local plants, mostly from our garden, and meat that Nathan and I kill ourselves. You're not still eating wheat, are you?"

"You really should not eat wheat," Nicky says.

The lectures begin. *Well that was quick*, thinks Sonia. Usually it takes at least a half hour before they start, not that she's seen her sister recently. It was all a distant memory but wow, how fast it all comes back to her now. Nicky and Steve, both oldest siblings, both bossy as all hell. "I pretty much eat everything that tastes good. That's my diet." She changes the subject. "Nathan hunts?" Sonia asks.

"I learned to shoot when I was six," Nathan says.

"How old are you now, Nathan?"

"I'm eight. I got a shotgun for my birthday. Do you want to see it?" He beams. "I got a smaller gun, too, for my seventh birthday. I could go out back and shoot a squirrel if you want."

"Finish your lunch first, Nathan," Nicky says.

"Is that even legal?"

"Colorado is pretty libertarian about these things," says Steve. He takes a delicate bite of quinoa bread and then examines the piece in his hand as if he's never seen it before in his life. "We think it's great for Nathan, teaching him gun safety and instilling our values."

Nathan moves around his dandelion salad in a way that Sonia recognizes as a way to make it appear he's eating. She envisions giving the poor kid a greasy piece of pizza, a bunch of Oreos.

"He's a good hunter," says Nicky.

Now, Sonia always knew that Nicky had become a full-on Western woman. She'd seen pictures of her on the occasional Christmas card, wearing a cowboy hat. Right now, she hears from another room, Good Lord, new country music playing softly. "Wow. That's pretty amazing." Sonia says. "My kids think guns only exist on television."

"We're going out bowhunting after lunch if you'd like to join us," says Steve before quickly correcting himself. "I guess in your condition that you might not want to."

"Steve, even if I wasn't pregnant, I would not go out bowhunting, but thank you anyway."

"I can't use the bow yet," says Nathan.

"It's too heavy for him, but not for long," says Steve. His pride is touching. He really loves his boy, Sonia can tell. She's trying to focus on things like that, instead of the fact that she finds fathers bonding with sons over killing things not only alien but unsavory.

"So, Sonia. Do you have an art show here or something?" Nicky asks. Of course Nicky can't imagine that Sonia would just come and visit her sister, and that's understandable because under normal circumstances, she wouldn't. But she's not normal right now. And the way Nicky said "art show" was typical Nicky, her disdain for Sonia's artistic ambition was a given. Sonia, the New York City artist. Except she's not really an artist, but even if she tried to explain that to Nicky, it wouldn't matter. Nicky's opinions have more to do with these set, cliché ideas in her head and very little to do with reality. In fact, she's never been to New York, so her idea of whatever it means that Sonia lives there is pretty much based on incorrect ideas that she holds dearly to herself. Not the most flexible person, her sister. Nor open-minded. Nor a good listener. But here they are.

"No, I wish." There's a silence then and Steve seems to get that Sonia wants to be alone with her sister. He and Nathan excuse themselves to prepare for the hunt.

"Let's go into the den," says Nicky, and Sonia follows her into a small room with a well-used beige couch, a rather dainty television set, a stereo, and an armchair in a Southwestern fabric, very Navaho-like. The walls are covered with pictures of Steve and Nathan smiling over the carcasses of dead animals. Sonia sinks deep into the armchair and her sister folds herself up on the couch.

"This room is great. So homey," says Sonia. "I'm loving my hotel, but it's not a home."

"What's going on, Sonia?"

"I left my family. Sort of abruptly."

"That's nuts."

"I feel nuts. This pregnancy is to blame."

"You've always been a bit nuts so I wouldn't blame the pregnancy entirely."

"I just needed to flee. So I did. I don't know. I've been frustrated with painting. Basically I haven't been painting."

"You have the rest of your life to paint, but your children are only young once."

Nicky never held back with her opinions and perhaps that was the one thing the two had in common, the often uncomfortable frankness of opinion.

"I know, I realize that. It's just that I'm happier when I'm painting. I think it makes me a better mother, when I'm happy with my work."

"Why the third baby then? I stopped with one and I don't even have a conflict with my 'art' or 'career' or anything."

"Like I said, it was an accident."

"So why didn't you get an abortion and then get your tubes tied? I mean, Sonia, leaving your family?"

"Well that didn't happen and here I am," Sonia says. "I was in South Bend before this. I stopped by the house. I saw Larissa and Larry, Dan's brother. Oh, and I stopped by the old house."

"How long have you been gone?"

"I've sort of lost track of time."

"It's the first week of January."

"I forget when I left. The end of November. Around there."

"Holy shit."

Steve and Nathan come in to say goodbye. Both of their faces are painted in shades of green and a terrible smell enters with them.

"You guys look like you're in *Apocalypse Now* and what is that smell?" asks Sonia.

"Oh, we rub elk urine on ourselves to attract the animals. Anyway, great seeing you. Will you be here when I get back?"

Nicky says, "Stay for dinner, Sonia."

"Um, that's nice of you," she tries to breathe through her mouth. "I might be here. Have a great time trying to kill things."

"I'll shoot a squirrel for you when we get back," says Nathan.

"That sounds great, Nathan," says Sonia. "See you later." A lingering odor remains after they leave and Sonia continues her mouth breathing.

"My life in New York is really different than this," Sonia says to her sister.

"I have no idea how you live in that hellhole," says Nicky, shaking her head in disbelief. "The taxes, the immigrants, the noise and filth. It makes you hate humanity not to mention how completely out of touch with nature you are. I think I'd die."

"I loved it at first, as you know," says Sonia.

"So you finally realized you're living in a den of horror," says Nicky.

"No, I wouldn't say that," says Sonia, thinking again of Steve's and little Nathan's painted faces and the stink of elk urine and thinks of *Apocalypse Now* and 'the horror,' "but it does wear on you, city life. I have no problem with paying my taxes or immigrants—which by the way, Nicky, is sort of racist and fucked up of you—but the noise and filth are harder to ignore than when I was younger."

"I'm not racist," Nicky says, and Sonia waits for the

self-deluding qualifier, and is not disappointed. "It's just," Nicky says, "the taking away of jobs that should go to Americans."

"Listen to yourself. Our mother was basically an immigrant. Let's just not go there right now. How is mom by the way? I have to call her and tell her I'm pregnant. I think she'll be happy for me."

"Just don't tell her you left your family and still didn't manage to visit her."

Sonia had thought of this. "I know, it's been ages since I visited them. With two little kids, traveling is really difficult."

"And now with the third, it's not going to get any easier. But anyway, she's doing well. I'm sure she'd love to hear from you."

Sonia wants to say something dismissive here, but weirdly, and somewhat out of character, bites her lip. She's always been envious of the easy nature of Nicky's relationship with her mother. Sonia's always felt her mother preferred Nicky, and why not? She knows she was a more difficult daughter.

"So, what are you going to do now? You must be close to your due date. Are you going to have the baby alone?"

"I haven't really thought about that."

"Sounds like you haven't done a lot of thinking at all," Nicky says.

Is this why she came out here? To have her sister be the bitch she always was? To confirm something she always knew about family life? That no matter how well inten-tioned parents are, their kids can grow up to be complete assholes to each other for no real reason other than that they're not the same? Often, in the years that she's raised her sons, she's thought, I'm going to raise them to love each other. And you know, it can happen. It just didn't happen with her and Nicky.

"Actually I've done a lot of thinking," Sonia says, aware that she's lying, and that she's really done more TV-watching and driving and learned how to push thoughts out of her head which turns out to be an amazingly wonderful, even practical, skill, "Just not about the practical things. It's been nice, not thinking practically. You should try it sometime. Free your mind, you know. When you were in college, you had a little hippie phase. Smoked some weed. Did some free thinking. It might do you some good."

"Well, I'm not in college anymore. I'm a grownup. You should try that sometime, acting like a grownup."

"Oh, I tried that. I thought it sucked. I gave it up years ago for Lent."

"Lent, huh? I thought you abandoned the church in high school? Are you going to church?"

"Yeah, yeah, I go to church. I go to church all the time." Sonia deadpans. "I go to church all the time, almost every-day. I love church. In fact, that's one the many things I've been thinking about, church. That and other things. I like thinking."

"Is this about your *art* again?"

Sonia sighs. "I don't know."

"You've been thinking about church and you don't know what else? Just 'things'?"

"I'm in transition."

"Haha, isn't that a term in labor, when you're about to push?" Nicky is now amused, Sonia sees. First she was baffled and judgmental, now she's just amused.

"You're right. I find that quite fitting."

"Well listen, Sonia, while you sit here thinking about church and things that you don't know what they are or whatever, I'm going for a run." Nicky stands up and starts stretching her calves.

"Didn't you shit yourself once doing that," Sonia asks.

"I shit myself when I ran an ultramarathon once," Nicky says defensively. "I'm just going on a ten-miler."

"Just a ten-miler."

"Yes, just a ten-miler."

"How long is an ultramarathon?"

"It was 36 miles."

"My God, well at least you only shat yourself as opposed to, I don't know, dying or something."

"You're welcome to stay for dinner. I have spare room upstairs if you want to nap."

"Thanks, Nicky. I'll think about it," Sonia says. "That's very nice of you. I may head back to the hotel. That way I can avoid watching a squirrel get shot."

"You know, I'm super proud of what a good little hunter Nathan is."

"I'm sure you are, it just seems sort of unnecessary to kill a rodent for fun."

"Oh, it's fun for him but we also eat everything we kill," Nicky says.

"You eat *squirrel*?"

"Sure. They're like chicken, only with less meat, more bones."

"I find that hard to believe. Can I use your bathroom?" Suddenly, Sonia has to pee in that pregnant way, right now or she'll pee herself.

Sonia puts a hand in her crotch and jogs to the bathroom and manages to not wet herself. Aaah. As she sits there peeing, she sees one of her mother's etchings. And she thinks, what's so bad about being an amateur artist, if it makes you happy? And it probably did make her mother happy. And the etching—of a woman with a child—is actually quite lovely, thinks Sonia. Sonia doesn't have any of her mother's etchings. Not one. She bets that Nicky has many. After she wipes herself and flushes, she takes down the framed etching and turns it around, trying to dismantle the frame. She leans the etching on the sink and digs away at the back and manages to free the etching.

"Are you OK in there?" asks Nicky, and Sonia's face goes hot.

"I'm fine," she says and adds a cough to hide the noise she's making.

"What's that noise? What are you doing?"

"Nothing!" Sonia coughs loudly. "I just have a cough."

Panicking now, Sonia puts the etching up her shirt, where it curves around her belly. She puts her hand on her belly and exits the bathroom, closing the door quickly behind her, and there is Nicky with her hands on her hips.

"What's in your shirt?" She's angry. She reaches for Sonia.

"Nothing! Nothing really," Sonia lunges away from her sister and Nicky tries again to grab for her. "Well, I'll just be going now, it was great seeing you," Sonia says as she jogs for the front door.

Nicky opens the bathroom door and sees the frame on the floor, says "Hey, you can't take that," and she starts after Sonia. "Mom made that just for me, after Nathan was born! Get back here, Sonia!"

Sonia is almost at the car now but Nicky's closing in on her fast. She gets the front door open and Nicky starts grabbing at her and Sonia throws some girly smacks at her.

"Jesus, Sonia, you're hitting me."

Sonia gets in and slams the door shut and presses the lock. Through the closed window, she screams, "Bye!" And backs down the drive. She's pretty sure she didn't tell Nicky which hotel she was staying at. And anyway, she just won't open her door. As she drives off, she reaches in and pulls out the etching, somewhat rumpled. She lays it on the passenger seat next to her, stealing glances at it. It is lovely, really lovely.

LATER, AT THE ST. Julien, Sonia sits at the bar in the elegant, grand lobby. A pianist plays classical music. Conversations take place at the carefully placed tables in the center of the room. She orders a steak and decides to not order wine. If she feared at first in Indiana that such a request could lead to her arrest, here she has no idea what to think. The bartender looks like a normal person—dark hair cut short, a good strong build, the classic white shirt and black pants of the waitstaff, but who knows, maybe he rubs urine on himself and eats squirrels. Sonia knows nothing. The steak is brought and she begins devouring it in a not so classy way.

"You look like you're enjoying that steak," a man says, sitting two seats away from her, a neat scotch in front of him. He's sort of red-faced, maybe ten years older than her.

Sonia pats her stomach, "Gotta feed the baby."

"Is it your first?"

"My third," Sonia says.

"What brings you to Boulder?" he asks. She likes the way he looks at her. Maybe he has a fetish for very pregnant women. They're out there, Sonia thinks. It takes all kinds.

"My sister lives here." Sonia says, with a little bit too

much steak in her mouth. She swallows before continuing, "Are you from here?"

"I'm from Denver. I'm here on business." He swallows his drink and the bartender refills it without him asking. "Real estate. I come here regularly."

"Well maybe you can explain to me why everyone seems so sporty and healthy and yet they're also like hippies, racist hippies, who don't want to pay taxes and . . ." Sonia turns to him, "Do you eat rodents?"

He laughs, "You sound like you're from New York."

"I am from New York," Sonia says. She shoves the last juicy bit of steak in her mouth and pushes her plate away. "That was a good guess."

"It wasn't so difficult, actually," he says. "Lots of New Yorkers come here." Sonia looks him in the eye, into his big brown puppy-dog eyes that seem a little glazed. He's drunk, but good at it. A pro.

"Do you have kids?"

"Two kids from my marriage. I'm divorced now. They're in college."

"Do you remember your wife being pregnant?" Sonia asks, thinking she can get some interesting information from him because he's drunk. He seems like a friendly drunk, but you never know, they can get nasty. But if that happens, she'll just go to her room.

"I do, of course. I remember the first one was a little overwhelming, for her and for me," he says.

"No shit. Did you guys have sex?" she asks.

He laughs. "Not at the very end." He drinks. "By the way, that's a very bold question."

"I'm researching pregnancy and families and what husbands think," she says.

"Are you a journalist?"

"No, I'm a sociologist," she says. Her lies are feeling really good. She should lie more often. She thinks about the lie she told on her way to Boston, about Dick being dead and the pity fuck she got out of that. "You say your first wife. Why'd you divorce? Did the stress of having children cause the divorce?"

"If you're doing research, how come you're not writing any of this down?" he asks.

"I have a photographic memory," she says. Sonia feels like getting a piece of chocolate cake and she orders one from the bartender.

"If you have a photographic memory, that means you remember what you see and we're just talking," he says. For a drunk guy, his brain works well. That must be because of the pro-quality vibe he gives off as a drunk person.

"Oh yes, I do have that, too," Sonia says, giving herself a fake little "silly me" knock on her forehead, "but I also remember everything people tell me. It's very useful in my line of work."

"That sounds really strange, to remember everything

people tell you. In fact it sounds like something out of a Borges story," he says.

"Well, Borges probably was inspired by meeting someone like me," Sonia says, faltering a bit. "His story had to come from someone, right?"

"I'm not so sure. But anyway, you asked about my marriage?" Sonia watches as the bartender refills his glass again. "Let's see, we were married for fifteen years. I don't think the stress of having children—which of course it is stressful—ruined our marriage. I don't think any one thing ruined our marriage. Frankly, the children kept us together more than anything else. What is more important in life than one's children?" he says and takes a drink with a sort of expertise. Clearly the man has lots of practice with drinking. "The children were our connection to each other, their future and health our greatest concern. As they got older and more independent, we had less of a connection, maybe. I don't know." Sonia now thinks that despite the drinking, he's a lot older than she thought at first, that he's well-preserved. "My wife started to feel a little lost as they got older. They had been the focus of her life and now they were at school all day, playing sports all afternoon, wanting to go to camp in the summers. She had a hard time adjusting. But that wasn't it, that wasn't the reason for our divorce. Or for our affairs."

"You both had affairs?" Sonia asks "Couldn't the children have pushed you to do that? I've found in my work, in researching for this study, that having children affects the sex life in a marriage."

"Sure, when the children are very little," he says, and he seems amused by Sonia and Sonia decides to like that rather than be annoyed. "But they don't stay little for long. And our sex life resumed pretty much. My memory isn't perfect. But your children are little so you don't know. You don't understand how things change. I do remember my wife, when she was taking care of the kids when they were little—it was as if she couldn't see into the future. The present was *so* strong, her daily life *so* all-encompassing. And then—boom—it was over. And by that I mean ten years later, or something like that. I don't remember how old they were, but one day I came back from work and she was sitting in her armchair, the same one she nursed the children in, held them in her lap when they were toddlers, and she was crying, just sitting there crying. I asked her what was wrong and she said, 'They're gone. They're gone and I'll never have them back. It's over. It's all over." I tried to convince her that wasn't the case—they were still living in our house, they were alive for God's sake, but in the next few days after that day, I realized she was right. We never would have a four-year-old again. A kindergartner. We'd never watch our own flesh and blood take his first steps. But that's not why we cheated on each other. Or maybe it sort of is." He finishes his drink. "Are you memorizing all of this?"

He smiles at her and Sonia thinks he's very attractive and normally she's not into older guys. Her fantasies tend to revolve around professional athletes in their twenties, which she knows isn't very creative of her. Maybe she's not creative after all, although she did have that cop fantasy. That was something new, and here she is finding this guy who is most likely in his fifties attractive. Then again, she is pregnant and she basically wants to have sex all the time, to the extent of not being as picky as she would be otherwise. "Yes, I am memorizing all of it." She points to her head. "It's all in here. I'll transcribe it later. You know, write it down word for word on my computer."

"You're a terrible liar," he says.

"I'm an excellent liar," Sonia says. "You wouldn't believe the things I've convinced people of. So did you get divorced because of the affairs?"

"I think I started having affairs because once I realized how fleeting it all is, how everything goes away and you can't have it back, I wanted to take advantage of everything I could. And that included having sex with women I wanted to have sex with, if they wanted to have sex with me. I assume my wife felt the same way, but I can't be certain. I would have forgiven her, taken her back or whatever, but that didn't happen."

"Why not?" Sonia asks, feeling panicky.

"There was just not enough love left. Love is something you have to nurture. Sort of like a plant. Or like anything.

You have to nurture your talents, your business. Your marriage, in particular the love part of the marriage. And we didn't do that."

"Well how can you if you're screwing someone else?"

"You can." The bartender pours him another drink and Sonia feels like she's getting a contact high just sitting near the man, smelling his scotch. "I've seen it done. But we didn't."

Silence. Sonia has no more questions. Suddenly, she's exhausted beyond all reason. "I have to go to bed," she says. "Thank you so much for contributing to my study. If you like, I'll mail it to you when it gets published."

He hands her a card. "You do that."

SONIA FALLS ASLEEP IN a daze. She sleeps on her side and normally she's not sleeping well, she never sleeps well when pregnant, which is a cruel thing considering that soon enough she'll be up all hours with a baby and really not sleeping well. And Sonia loves sleep, always has, more than most people. She is not the kind of person who is up at the crack of dawn. But this night, she sleeps well, dreamlessly, and it's noon before she props herself up to call room service. After calling room service, she calls Dick at work.

"Hi, it's me," she says.

"Sonia?"

"Yeah, it's me. Happy New Year."

"I'm in a meeting, one sec," he says. She hears him make excuses and pictures him walking into the hallway, leaving a conference room.

"What on earth?" he says. "Why are you calling me?"

"Did you get my postcard?"

"I got it," he says.

"I'm in Boulder and I'm coming home," she says. "It's going to take a while. I have to stop a lot. Driving hurts my body like you wouldn't believe."

"Just get on an airplane."

I'm not going to do that."

"Get on an airplane, Sonia. We can get the car later. We can hire someone to drive it back."

"Dick, I'm heading east today. Just give me some more time."

"More time? *More* time?"

"You being pissy isn't going to make me drive any faster or change my mind."

"Don't you care at all?" he says and she feels bad she called him at work, he's so emotional. "About your own children? About . . . *us*?"

"I do. That's why I'm heading back."

"Why won't you get on a plane? Believe it or not, you're needed here."

"Nicky's son kills squirrels with a small gun and then they eat them," Sonia says, because why not try to change the subject?

"That's nice, Sonia. Come home."

"I'm coming," she says. "Bye." And she hangs up and wonders, how awful will it be? Or will it not be awful? Why won't she get on a plane? She gets up, takes a long warm bath in a beautiful pristine bathtub, a tub that in no way resembles the tub in Brooklyn. She thinks, feed the love. Nurture the love. How hard can that be?

19

Holiday Inn Expresses. Ramada Inns. A few Hiltons and not very nice ones. She now has a neck pillow she shoves behind her lower back, to ease the pain. Everything feels bad. Her ankles swell. It's hard to reach the pedals and the wheel what with her belly in the way, and she hates it when her belly pushes up against the wheel, so her arms are outstretched and this tires them immensely. But she makes it to Wisconsin, and hours later, without calling first, she is driving to Philbert's house. There is snow everywhere. Big piles of it. The road is pretty clean, but still. Snow, more snow, and then some more snow. Clean, country snow, unlike in Brooklyn. No yellow dog pee, candy wrappers, beer cans. Indeed, this snow has that sparkle to it, crystals refracting the light.

How could it be that he was listed like that? It was very unlike him, or her memory of him. But Philbert Rush would always be Philbert Rush. Surly, a bit paranoid, arrogant, gleefully vicious. As an infant—he'd told her this once—he screamed constantly, and thrashed about in his mother's arms. Born raging. And yet, when Sonia calls information in Wisconsin—where she knew he'd moved from calling the Boston Museum School, a nice, young receptionist saying, he's teaching at the University of Wisconsin—all she has to do is ask for Philbert Rush, and she's given his phone number, as well as the route and town he lives in.

Phil Rush. "Outsider" artist, but of course, sought after because of his aloofness. Sonia always found that annoying. After ten years in New York he left—claiming no real art could ever be made in New York, that society destroys the artist. This, after conveniently spending enough time in society to secure Sonnebende as his venue for exhibition. So he moved to Boston where Sonia met him in his drawing class. His classes were famous because he rarely had anything nice to say to the students and all the students loved him for that.

On Sonia's first day of class with Phil, she stood near the front, which was her way. A plumpish, breasty girl with red streaks dyed into her long brown hair was the model. She was beautiful, in that way that young women are, flawlessly fresh and round and she imbued the class with a sexual tension. Ten minutes into the class, Phil stood behind Sonia and she could smell him. It wasn't a good or a bad smell, just a distinct, human odor. A salty, slightly sour smell. (Once she'd tried to paint how he smelled, for fun, at her studio in Boston. That one she threw out.)

He stood behind her on that first day, his arms crossed, his dark brow screwed into a deep V above his long, thin nose, his black hair standing straight up around his head as if he'd stuck his finger in a light socket.

He said, "You call that an arm? That is your idea of an arm? Where is the poetry in it? Where is the life? Throw that out. Throw it out and start over. God!" Shortly thereafter, she started fucking him.

He never let her spend the night. After dozing for a while on the floor, in the bed, wherever they'd landed, she'd get up, get dressed, and leave. He'd already be back in his studio. Fuck and paint. That's what the man did. No matter what time of the day or night it was.

THE SKY IS DARK and she is nearly sweating from her copious body fat and the heat pouring out of the vents, but also, she knows it is cold out and this alone chills her blood. Fucking freezing cold dark Midwestern bleakness. Unending. And yet it does end, at least the trip part. She reaches a long, winding gravel driveway through some pine trees blanketed in a dull gray-white frozen snow and then—his house. An unassuming, wood-framed modern house. An outbuilding nearby in a cleared part of the woods that must be his studio. And everywhere else: purity, serenity,

simplicity, seclusion. All of his concentration and flam-
boyance and originality reserved for the grueling, exalted
transcendent calling. Sonia looks around and thinks, this
is how I will live. Someday. Not now, not for ten years or
more, but someday, this is how I will live. The sound of
the wind on the icy trees sounds akin to the shriek of nails
on a chalkboard. Before she knocks, he opens the door.

"You're not invited. What are you doing here?" He
stares at her with his lyrical almond eyes, his kissable
expressive underlip firmly annoyed.

"I need to talk to you."

"I should turn you away. My God. You are enormously
pregnant." His voice, deep but slightly grating. It's as if he
never could get rid of his Newark upbringing despite the
sixty years spent trying.

"Let me in. You make yourself so easy to be found."

"No one tries to find me here in Wisconsin. So I have
no reason to make myself hard to find."

"If you don't want me to accidentally give birth here on
your steps, then invite me in to sit down."

He walks in the house and Sonia follows.

"Give birth on my front step. I love it. Rich. I could use
that image, you know."

THERE IS VERY LITTLE furniture. There is no couch. It is an
ascetic environment, one created so he can work. It is not a
home, really. It is a place where a man gets sustenance so he

can work. A place to eat and sleep. Large, dark, abstract can-
vases lean against the walls. Rothko, without the color. The
texture is thick. They are beautiful. How can something
so simple take so much work? So much dedication? And
yet, Sonia knows, it does. Sonia, exhausted and with intense
back pain throws herself on the only comfortable looking
piece of furniture she sees, a strange, black leather, S-shaped
chair, a midcentury design. It's not so uncomfortable. She
starts, immediately, to tell him things. The boys at home.
Her ambivalence. Even how she'd hoped to start painting
again before this pregnancy began, and as the words come
out, she's hears their lameness. The falseness and meekness
of her words. And she can't stop herself. She's making more
excuses, they're churning in her brain now.

"I went on a road trip. I went to Boston and then back to
Indiana, and then out West, to visit my sister."

"You hated Indiana. And your sister."

"I know, but it's where I grew up. I needed to go back
for some reason."

"And what reason would that be?"

Sonia thinks about getting high and the gum art. "It was
a good thing, it's good to revisit our pasts. You should try it
some time. When was the last time you were in Newark?"

He ignores her, turning his back to her, picking up
something from a side table.

"Anyway, this pregnancy has me—has affected me—oh,
I don't know."

She says, to her shame and embarrassment and really, to set herself up, "I know I'll love this baby. When it comes. So I try and comfort myself with that."

Now he's back to looking at her. God, his attention. How she desired it so much, just to have him pay attention to her. "I don't doubt that you'll 'love' your baby. What- ever that means. You are so ridiculous, you know that? 'I know I'll love this baby,'" he says, nastily, mimicking her, sitting across from her and taking her in. "I see it in your eyes, that hope. The thrill of it. You are no better than a ten-year-old girl, wanting to go on the roller-coaster ride just one more time, and eat just one more bag of cotton candy. And there will be fun in it, in the excessiveness, but you may also throw your guts up. The suffering may out- weigh the pleasure. And of course, you are not ten. It's not your stomach and mind that is at stake. It's other people's lives. Other people's fucking lives that you are messing with. Your two sons, the daughter that's on her way, your husband, who it seems you don't even give a fuck about. And yet, you walk this earth, travel this country, acting as if you are some holy person. Some Madonna. A mother! A mother-to-be! You want respect, you want to be treated well. You think you are doing this world a favor. But really, every day, and every child you choose to have—and I wouldn't put it past you to keep on going after this third, by the way—is just you avoiding taking a long hard look at the failure you are. And the misery you have created. Hey, focus on a new one and then you won't have to look at the mistakes you made the first and second times around!

"And there are many problems with this. First, you walk around with no truth. This kills your soul. You walk around, presenting yourself as someone that you are not, doing things, creating life, like God, but you are a false God, because you do not admit why you are doing what you are doing. To yourself, maybe the truth whispers itself to you, a tiny bit, at night sometimes. But you ignore it, and go about in the world as a complete lie. Your public life is a lie, and so your inner life, your soul, your chance to commune with God, is gone. And you call yourself a mother, like this is a good thing, something to be proud of, something that deserves respect. And you appear fit to be a mother, in the eyes of all the other liars you walk around the earth with. God! God help us all!"

Sonia feels one with the S-shaped chair. She thinks it's actually made for pregnant women. Or maybe, it's made so that a pregnant woman can never get up from it. The thought of getting up seems impossible. And the view of Philbert, as he walks slowly around—entrances her. She says. "Actually, I don't appear fit to be a mother anymore. I've left my family. And a friend called social services on me. Or someone who used to be a friend."

"You'll go back. You'll keep playing the charade. You'll slime your way back into it. I don't doubt that for a minute."

This is what he says to her, after letting her into his home. Her back is relaxed now—this is so much better than the car—her legs up on the curve of leather, a cup of water in her hand.

He gets up and walks away from Sonia, he turns his glowing black eyes away, and for a moment she can really breathe. The air comes in, the air goes out. She looks at the back of his head and it is virtually a nest, gray and black dreadlocks crisscrossing about in a thick clump, with rivers and valley forming in the mass. *Animals live in that hair*, thinks Sonia, *on his scalp, feasting on the flesh of his head*. He disappears into another room and she can hear water run. Hear the click of a gas stove being turned on.

Her mouth is dry despite the water. What she really needs to do is drink oil. She is so happy to see this man. This was what the whole trip was about. Seeing him. And she hadn't known that until now.

She says, "I love my children. I love having children. We are biologically programmed to have children. I became fixated on it at a certain point and I have no regrets. You call yourself an adult and you question my maturity to bring children in the world and yet someone took a chance and gave birth to you. You, who's never humbled yourself to be a parent. Because being a parent is about humility. And about not being so self-absorbed anymore. Humility is a good thing. Even in the face of art. You think you'd be out here in fucking Wisconsin if you had kids? Fuck.

You'd be the most famous painter in New York. Your art would have transcended itself. You would have been more of a person, and therefore, more of an artist. You're just bitter. And wrong. Not having children is like not passing puberty. Not having children is like not ever getting a job. It is, it is all that . . . and so much more. Not having children is missing the most sacred transition in life, from child to adult. It's like not dying, like not being born. It is missing the most important stage in life on this planet, the only real stage between birth and death, the two stages that are forced upon us."

He sits down in front of her on a stool, holding a warm cup in his hands.

"You, you who once believed in free will. You think I don't remember that about you? I remember things about you because you once had promise. Now you don't. I look at you and I see it in your eyes. You belong in front of the TV. You belong on a park bench, you belong humped over a stove, cooking a disgusting box of macaroni and cheese. You are over. Your mind is gone. You have no light in your face. None. That wasn't always the case, you know."

"How dare you judge me now! I'm pregnant. I'm in a state of change. This is not the permanent me. This is me right now and very soon I won't be pregnant anymore. The minute this baby drops out of me, I'll be different. I'll get a part of me back." Sonia's eyes tear with rage.

"A part of you back? And the rest? Where's the rest go?

Into those hungry mouths, all three of them. You choose to raise them, you choose to not have a life. It's that simple. My mother . . ."

"Don't fucking talk to me about your mother." She spits out, interrupting him. "We are talking about me and I'm not your mother. Not all mothers are the same. To be a mother isn't to be like all mothers."

"Fair enough. But you are the one who brought up biology. We are not biology, Sonia, you fool. We live in a time where we have technologies to make choices. You chose to have kids."

"I realize that."

"And this talk of humility. What is that? That humility can only be experienced by a parent?"

"A certain kind of humility, yes, I think can only be experienced by a parent." She puts both her hands on her stomach. The baby feels her agitation. It's moving, visibly too, she looks down and can see her stomach move, and her hands feel it and a part of her wants Philbert to feel it, how amazing it is, to have a growing human inside you.

"Must you make it a special club, with special privileges, is that the only way to survive this horrible thing, being a mother? Pretend it's something that it's not? And you contradict yourself. Not all mothers are the same. But all mothers experience profound humility. So that is sameness. And so then I am right. And I have every right to compare you to my mother. You know what humility did to her? It made her nothing. It made her a sorrowful, bored, and mediocre person. She will get into heaven easily, but at what cost?"

"You don't believe in heaven, Phil, remember? And humility doesn't have the same effect on everyone. I am humble in front of my canvas. How's that? I worship art like you will never experience. I need it more now than ever before, I need it for an escape from my life. You, you don't know what need is. Your whole fucking life is a luxury. I need art. You just live it. Just wait. Just stick around. You'll see."

"You and canvas? What canvas? When was the last time you were in front of a canvas?"

She'd told him she hadn't been painting. She regretted that now. "The fucking canvas of my mind is rich. And soon enough, I'll be in front of a real one. So I don't get to be a young artist. Fine. But I'm going to start painting the minute this baby is out of me. So I don't get to be a young artist."

"You were once. You gave that up."

"Youth is overrated in art. We might look better in the magazines, but very few people make interesting art before their forties." Sonia had thought these very thoughts before, when Tom was born. When Mike was born. But then, it had been thirties, not forties, that had been the time when artists become interesting.

"Yes, you'll start painting and later, I'll be young again. I'll be able to fuck like I used to fuck! Like I used to fuck you." He smiles at her and even though ten years have passed, she realizes he hasn't changed, despite his admitting he couldn't fuck like he used to. He retains some sharpness, something youthful, that she knows is gone in her. He looks like sex—how men his age could do that, amazes her. His crazy hair, his eyes so alive, his lips hanging from his mouth, the memory of those lips on her. She'd fuck him in a heartbeat, although she could just imagine he would never, ever fuck a pregnant woman. "Painting isn't something you can just pick up later. You used to know that once. You used to know more than you know now. I agree that as an artist ages, for the most part, his work becomes more interesting, but he must first go through all the early stuff, through it in art. Just being twenty or thirty isn't enough. One must be creating and learning through that time, even if you are just producing a ton of crap."

He sips his tea delicately perched on his stool. He has delicate but strong hands. He holds the teacup like an English society girl. "You've become stupid about art. Delusional. Maybe you need those delusions—you must. Pretend that you'll get it all back, that drive, that need. The talent. Like talent isn't something that needs so much nurturing."

"There are no rules, Phil. You taught me that. *You've* become stupid about art, because that is all you have. You are blinded to the rest of the world, you have no perspective."

"I have a life, you fool. I have more than my art. I have friends, I have lovers. I have this home and these woods that surround it. I have music to listen to, fine wine to drink. I have so much. But my life feeds my art, it doesn't take away from it. That is the difference between you and me. My life is set up to inspire me. To accommodate my creativity. To nurture me. Who nurtures you? Who gives you anything? Don't tell me your kids, the ones you've abandoned. They take and take and take. And what are you going to do with that? Suck the life out of them later? Mothers do that. They think they can get it all back later."

"You ass."

"You are so miserable I can barely stand to look at you. You are so full of lies. Your children, your children. The world doesn't need your children. The world doesn't want your children."

"Oh, and the world really needs your art. Your fucking paintings. That is what the world needs." She is so angry at him. She used to think the world needed his art. Needed art period.

"Ah, but here is the difference. Here is the truth, something you once knew something about, truth. I *know* what I do is a privilege, a construct. I don't carry myself like a God or like a vessel of Nature. I don't ever pretend that what I am doing is something sacrificial, something good. The good artist. The good mother. My life isn't a lie."

Sonia starts crying a bit now and it feels good. "My life is not a lie."

"Your whole life must be a lie, or else you would be in jail for child abuse. You brought them here by fucking your husband. And that is something that you will lie to them about your whole life. You'll pretend that you brought them here because you wanted them. That you, the mother, never committed some atrocious, mucousy, animal act and they were the accidental product of it. Unless, of course, you let them know that, and then, of course, you'd be a very sick woman indeed."

Confused, tears running down her face, Sonia feels like she's being bathed in his hate. "We grow up, we realize our parents had sex. It doesn't kill us."

"No, but pretending to be something we are not does kill us. You are the one who will be dead. You already are dead, in many ways."

"I will not die, Phil. I will live a double life. I do already. And that is the real truth. It is. It really is. Bothness. The love and the hate. The mucous fuck and the tender innocent cheek of the baby. I will have it all and it won't kill me because I'll know the truth. Even if I can't walk around saying it as I buy diapers and cookies at the store. There is public life and private life. I didn't create the two things. There is an inner life and an outer life. There are layers and layers of ourselves. To be one thing is not to *not* be another."

"What happened to the Sonia who couldn't stand hypocrisy? Who felt she would burst if she pretended to like someone she didn't like, who turned bright red and hyperventilated in the presence of all that social bullshit? Now you are a sorority girl, yes? And that is OK? It's not going to kill your soul? Now that you can look like one thing and be another? What happened to your sensitivity? How do you think you'll make art if you lost that?"

Sonia's hands still lay on her belly. The baby has settled. The sense of this person inside of her has become more real to her now than ever before. She runs her hands from the bottom of her belly to the top and then stretches them over her head.

"A thicker skin won't kill my soul. Maybe it'll protect it. So I don't walk around with my heart exposed to the world quite as much. I still have a heart. I do, I do."

"I haven't noticed it. I don't sense its presence." He smiles wickedly at her. He puts the tea to his lips, and warm smoke from the cup rises in his face.

"You didn't offer me tea. You bastard. You make yourself tea and don't offer me any."

He laughs a big, hearty laugh. The sound of it makes Sonia cry again, freshly, tears of joy. To hear his nasty laugh! The sound of it!

"I didn't invite you here. You show up at my doorstep, uninvited. And then you expect me to nurture you. You make yourself tea. And me some more, too. That's how things work here."

SONIA LURCHES HER HUGE, unbalanced body out of the S-shaped chair and hurls herself out of Phil's house. It's dark now, but the moon is so intense, the stars too, that everything glows, everything is visible. There's a light on in the outbuilding, the studio. She stumbles in the snow as she heads toward it. The snow is nearly knee deep and her feet get immediately wet and cold as she trudges through it. She falls forward and as she rights herself, she looks down and sees the imprint of her stomach in the snow. Her snow angel, a big round circle, space enough to put a dead baby deer. Huffing—just breathing is so hard now that the baby is so big and taking up so much space—she manages to get to the outbuilding, which on closer inspection is an old, small barn, lovingly restored and painted dark brown. Phil is coming behind her. He's yelling, "What the fuck do you think you're doing? I don't let just anybody in my studio!"

And Sonia grabs for the door, trying to open it. But it's locked with a padlock. The wind sears her face and Phil's coming toward her now, a key in his hand. He's grinning and his hair whips upward in a huge black spiral, like Medusa, like a band of snakes, as the wind threatens to blow them both down.

"You want in there?" He yells over the noise of the wind.

"You thief! You want to steal my soul. You would if it were possible. Anything, right? Anything to get what you want? You'd stop at nothing."

And he's right. She needs to steal his soul, as she's lost her own. And she lunges at him, her hand, for a moment, on his wrist. He's all teeth and silent laughter now, his head thrown back, and she reaches and reaches again, but he's quicker. He moves his hand up and then to the left and then to the right. She's frantically grabbing, but he moves too fast. She falls again, sinking, knee-deep in the snow. She reaches, but he's taller and more able. And he's not pregnant.

At last she stops herself. Grunting, she tries to stand, but can't. She has fallen. The snow, the cold, her huge body. She lies there in the dark and the white. He looms above her, the man she most wanted to be.

She can barely make out his face. But it's him.

20

February 8

"Were you here in this hospital the whole time? Why were you here?" Tom asks Sonia, a look of perplexed wonder on his beautiful face. She can't believe how much she missed her boys. And how much he seems to have grown.

"No, sweetie," Sonia says, "I wasn't here the whole time. Do you want to hold your baby sister?"

"Ok!" Tom says. Sonia passes the baby to her older boy and she remembers doing the same thing when Mike was born and what a moment it was, one of those you take with you to your grave. He's too little to do this on his own, really, and Dick supervises next to him on the couch, making sure he holds his sister's head upright. She feels and sees the emotion brimming in Dick and it's so different than when her sons were born, so much more complicated, his hurt mixed in with the rest of it. He looks exhausted and she's the one who just gave birth. But he looks exhausted on some cellular level that a week of good night sleeps probably won't help. And there she is staring at her husband, her son, her newborn daughter. The absolute richness of life floors her and she has to look away.

"She's ugly, Mommy," Tom says, apologetic, sort of whispering.

"She's just brand new. She'll get prettier, I promise."

"Daddy said you were on a long vacation. It was too long, Mommy."

"I know. I got lost on my way back. I'm sorry. But I'm back now," Sonia says. She tries to make eye contact with Dick, looking for some support, some idea of what he's thinking. She's not even sure what she's thinking, how much damage she's done. She just wants to be all together, at home. The thought of another hotel room, even this hospital, she can't bear it. And she can't do this on her own. She needs Dick. Dick avoids her eyes and Sonia thinks that's OK, that at least he's here, he came to Philadelphia when she called. Regardless: shame, remorse, and a general confusion flood her, and she leans back on the hospital bed and closes her eyes.

"Don't go to sleep, Mommy." Mike says, who grew so much in just two months, crawling up in the bed with her. She can barely look at him. She trembles. Will they ever forgive her? Or will they barely remember the time their mother left them and came back with a baby? She hopes for the latter. Hell, she only remembers things like getting her finger slammed in the car door or the time her dad accidentally ran over a cat. Big events. Maybe her absence was a sort of a nonevent, maybe not. It wasn't the bloody kind of painful. People used to leave their children all the time. If they had to. And they still do. Sonia thinks of all those Tibetan nannies she met once, whose children remained in India while they took care of white people's children in Park Slope, not seeing their own children for years. Of course, they had few choices. Whereas Sonia's whole life was one choice after another, some she knew to be bad at the time, some that felt good, but, looking back, were really bad. And then there were the good choices, she thinks, looking at her newborn daughter, feeling the warmth of Mike's skin against her, his little bones poking into her still delicate, ripped-open body. He's hurting her a bit, but she can't push him away.

"I'm not sleeping, just closing my eyes for a minute. Soon Daddy's going to take you two to get something to eat and then soon after that, we'll drive back home. Won't that be nice?"

Later, in the car, driving back to Brooklyn, the boys buckled up and falling asleep, not in car seats (which thankfully Dick hasn't said anything about), their sister in a new infant car seat between them, Sonia reminding herself that for a million years no one used car seats, that Dick was a good, safe driver, and, trying not to think of the other bad drivers out in the world, she turns to Dick.

She says, awkwardly—or forcing herself to put the awkwardness in her voice, because, in spite of her anxieties, she feels quite natural saying what she's about to say, as though, somehow, everything is back as before—"Thanks for coming to get me."

"I came to get my daughter, too."

"I suppose you're going to be an asshole too, for some time."

Dick still doesn't look at her. "I suppose."

"Well, that probably can't be helped."

"Probably not."

Then a silence. And her feeling of naturalness crumbles. What does she expect? A warm welcome? Hugs and kisses? She abandoned her family. She's an idiot in so many ways but she's not delusional. The warmth of other bodies. Intimacy. Life seems so meaningless without them.

Sonia says, "She's beautiful, the little girl. We have to name her." She thinks she sees tears in Dick's eyes. They have a baby, a new baby and nothing in the entire world is more remarkable.

"Was it worth it, Sonia?" he says quietly. She checks that the boys are still sleeping. She says, "I have no fucking idea, Dick. No idea. But it's over. And to me, that's all that matters. I'm where I belong even if I don't feel like I belong. But I'm done fighting it. Believe me."

"I don't believe you. I can't trust you."

"Well, we'll just have to muddle through. I mean, do you want to move out, or have me move out?"

"I'm tired. I don't know. No. I asked you to come home, remember. I'm"—he looks so hurt, Sonia has to look away—"just really angry at you."

"I'm happy to see you," Sonia says. And she is: his thinning hair, his narrow jaw, his broad shoulders. All of it. Everything about him warms her right now. He's her husband, the father of her three children. They're together now, as they should be. "I just lost it. I'm better now. Now that she's outside of me. Or something. And I need you, Dick."

"I hate you when you're pregnant."

"Well maybe you should be grateful I left you then!" Sonia is only sort of joking. "I hate me when I'm pregnant, too. Or at least, it changes me. And not all for the better. But it's over now, Dick. And she's so beautiful." Sonia looks back at her baby girl. She couldn't be any prouder, any more in awe, any more high with exhaustion.

Dick says nothing. And they drive home like that, silently, until the baby starts to cry.